LOVE BY THE FIRE

Rosalind, her emotions raw after her encounter with the man she had fled long years before and just now, her nerves tried after her narrow escape from the sea, could be brave no longer. She buried her face in the Viscount's perfect cravat and sobbed as if her heart would break.

Moreland, astonished but overjoyed to feel her arms convulsively clasping him, was momentarily powerless to do more than hold her and let the sensations triggered by her nearness wash over him. Without speaking, his lips against her hair, he held her as the storm in her broke around them . . . With a gentle touch, he lifted her face to his. The firelight played across her tear-marked face, and he wondered if he would ever see firelight without thinking of her.

AG

Daring Illusion

Christina Cordaire

JOVE BOOKS, NEW YORK

DARING ILLUSION

A Jove Book / published by arrangement with
the author

PRINTING HISTORY
Jove edition / April 1994

ISBN: 0-515-11362-X

A JOVE BOOK®
Jove Books are published by The Berkley Publishing Group,
200 Madison Avenue, New York, New York 10016.
JOVE and the "J" design are trademarks belonging
to Jove Publications, Inc.

PRINTED IN THE UNITED STATES OF AMERICA

10 9 8 7 6 5 4 3 2 1

Chapter 1

"Andy! You cannot be serious!"

Andromeda Winston, eldest remaining child of the sixth Earl of Winston, took a quick turn about the small stone-paved alcove in the rose garden. Her dark curls bounced as she rounded on her siblings. "Indeed I *am* serious! I have thought and thought, but I simply cannot find any other solution."

Andromeda's twin, Perseus, raked his fingers distractedly through curls only slightly shorter than her own, his deep blue eyes regarding her seriously from an extraordinarily handsome face. He was frowning. "I say, Andy. That's a pretty *drastic* solution, isn't it?"

Andromeda, perfect proof against his brooding beauty, since it was merely the masculine echo of her own, retorted, "Drastic situations demand drastic solutions!"

"Well, I'll tell you one thing, my girl. We're going

1

to need at least one person who is older. How are you going to manage *that* little detail, pray tell!"

"With Hermes dead, there are no 'adults' left in the family. You know that as well as I do, Pers," she said, trying not to cry.

A young voice piped up, "There's Rosalind."

"They didn't hear you, Castor," Pollux said with a heavy sigh. "They never hear us."

"Well," his identical twin answered, "there *is* Rosalind. She was married to our brother Hermes, so that makes her old."

"And she was sooo pretty, too."

"And nice." Castor hugged himself in pleasant memory.

Andromeda snapped at the younger twins, annoyed as only sweet sixteen can be to hear twenty-two called old. "We have no idea where Rosalind is, Gemini." She used the family short form of address for them. "Now hush." She turned back to Perseus. "That is a mere detail. It's the plan as a whole I intend that you shall accept."

Fifteen-year-old Cassiopeia, the only blond member of the dark-haired Winston clan, spoke hesitantly from where she perched beside the younger twins. Anything was better than letting the older twins get into one of their famous brangles. "You're looking positively mulish, Andromeda. I hope your mind is not *absolutely* made up, dear." She twisted her handkerchief into an unrecognizable knot.

Andromeda was certain she could hear the embroidery threads pop even above the sound of the surf far below the secluded, sun-warmed terrace. The knowledge that her sister Cassie had just wasted another expensive scarf of linen did nothing to alleviate her present sour mood. "Don't be a widgeon, Cassie Winston. You—all of you—must get it through your heads. There are simply *no* funds. And there haven't been since our parents were killed in the carriage accident. None! Neither to keep Castle Winston open *nor* to support us in a less elaborate setting."

She was driven by desperation. She must make them see! "You know Papa gambled away every penny! My plan is the only way open to us. *And*"— she glowered at each of her brothers and sisters in turn as she said with slow and threatening emphasis—*"you had better get used to my idea. Every last one of you!"*

"Yes, I understand the plan, Moreland. But how the devil do you think you can insinuate yourself into life on that coast?" The speaker, retired General Sir Richard Attleborough, grasped his own short gray beard and gave it a tug, for all the world as if he would thus pull his next thought into being. "As far as I can remember, lad, you have no holdings in that area."

"No, I haven't." Viscount Moreland shifted languidly in his chair. His casual posture belied the crackling intelligence in his eyes. "Blast it! When I think of the numerous estates with which I'm saddled, I can't help wishing that one of my forebears might have had the foresight to provide me with just *one* that would be of assistance to England in the present crisis."

"Ah, well, Moreland." Attleborough made a vague gesture meant to reassure. "They cannot have foreseen this, you know. Can't have foreseen it." A document caught his eyes, and the gesture ended in his picking up a paper from the crowded surface of his desk. His voice became faint as his attention settled on the paper. "You'll find a way. You always do."

Before he lost his superior's attention entirely, Moreland asked quickly, "May I have Lytton, sir?"

"Lytton? Yes, yes. No good here the way he is. Been a waste of time the two months he's been home. Done nothing but mope since he lost that arm. Take him . . . I wish you joy of him."

Rising, Moreland bowed, squared his wide shoulders, and turned away from his superior's desk. He knew he'd been forgotten before his hand touched the doorknob to let himself out of the spacious room.

Moments later he left the War Office. All too soon, thanks to the excellent servants in his employ, he would arrive at his palatial London home and be forced to come to grips with the thorny problem that awaited him there—his sister, Valerie.

He smiled grimly, not entirely without a certain ironic humor. He wondered if his superior would be shocked to know that the problem he'd left behind paled in comparison to the one before him. Somehow, since Attleborough was said problem's godfather, Moreland was certain he would not be in the very smallest bit surprised.

"Mrs. Winston!" The stout matron fairly vibrated with indignation as she addressed the slender widow of the valiant Captain Hermes Winston standing calmly in front of her. "Do you actually mean to stand there and tell me that you expect me to believe that you did nothing to lure my poor, dear Alfonse into your web?"

Lady Rosalind, Countess Winston, met the eyes of her employer unflinchingly. "I have not *in any way* encouraged your son to think he may force his unwanted attentions on me, Mrs. Ledbetter, I assure you. Furthermore, I am your younger children's governess, not a spider, and therefore have no web."

Alfonse stood behind his mother's chair and watched with malice glittering in his eyes. Rosalind was certain the disgusting little toad was enjoying seeing her receiving a scold from his overindulgent mama. How any but the most indulgent mother could deceive herself into thinking that any woman would encourage advances from Alfonse was beyond her!

"We'll have none of your insolence, if you please, Mrs. Winston! I hired you to teach my two little girls out of the kindness of my heart—you being the widow of one of our brave boys fighting Napoleon and all. But I hold no truck with lewd behavior. Even though I realize that once having enjoyed the marriage bed—"

"*Mrs. Ledbetter!*" Rosalind was certain her outraged cry could be heard in every nook and cranny of the Ledbetters' tasteless redbrick monstrosity of a house, and probably out in the street besides.

The ample matron had the grace to blush at her ill-chosen words. After all, the marriage bed was hardly a subject for discussion in mixed company, let alone for those of tender years.

Her blush of shame soon turned to a flush of anger, however. Anger she was quick to turn on the hapless woman standing so straight and proud before her. "That's neither here nor there, Mrs. Winston. The subject at hand is your own unacceptable behavior in luring a boy of my Alfonse's age to your room in the middle of the night."

"I did no such thing." Rosalind's words were firm, her chin high and her gaze unflinching. She had no doubt that she was about to be dismissed. Undoubtedly without a recommendation. She sighed inwardly. She could do without that, as she knew she could always get one from any of her childhood friends, but she suspected that the cheese-paring Mrs. Ledbetter was about to use Alfonse's lie as a justification for doing her out of her just wages, as well. And those she couldn't do without.

She hadn't long to wait to see.

"I suppose you think you should be compensated for the time you've spent trying to seduce my sweet boy."

Alfonse was grinning openly now behind his mother's back.

"Indeed, I do not! I have spent not one moment doing anything about your Alfonse, other than attempting to avoid him. I have, however, spent considerable time trying to drum some learning into the heads of your girls and to teach them to *overcome their upbringing* to some extent by instructing them in social graces." She ignored Mrs. Ledbetter's explosive. "Well! I never!" and went on. "It is for that Herculean labor that I expect to be paid."

Lips compressed, twin warning flags of high color in her cheeks, she turned blazing eyes on the matron before her. "And if I am not, I shall return to

Mrs. Findlay at the Registry that put me in your employ and tell her exactly what has transpired here." Fearlessly she faced her employer, her fine gray eyes flashing.

"You . . . you . . ." Mrs. Ledbetter seemed to be having trouble coming to grips with the emotion she was experiencing. "You cannot be saying that you would hope to be believed over *my* word!"

"Indeed, I assure you I am saying just that." Rosalind turned so swiftly her skirts made a sound like a sword cutting the air. Looking back over her shoulder at Mrs. Ledbetter, she commanded, "Please have my wages ready in one half hour. I am sure that will be ample time for me to pack and to say 'good-bye' to the few people I hold in esteem in this household."

"Now, see here! Why should I believe that Mrs. Findlay or anyone else at her Domestic Registry would take *your* word about anything that happened under this roof to a mere governess?" Mrs. Ledbetter's vindictive voice was showing the strain of the moment. Not only was she outraged, she was probably feeling she had been bested.

"Because . . ." The imperious Mrs. Winston hesitated for a moment in the doorway of the horrible, bright green morning room to confirm her employer's worst fears. "Because," she repeated in a voice icy with calm, "in her youth, Mrs. Findlay, God bless her, was *my* governess!"

Mrs. Ledbetter and Alfonse stared at the space through which the regal Mrs. Winston had swept for a long moment. Then Mrs. Ledbetter rose slowly from her chair, turned, and slapped her son hard enough to rock his stocky figure before she went to her desk to procure the highly unsatisfactory Mrs. Winston's scanty wages.

No one seeing Edward Forsythe, Eighth Viscount of Moreland, descend from his coach and enter his impressive town house, would have guessed that the handsome gentleman felt anything but glad to be home. He moved with athletic grace, his form elegant, his clothing obviously from the finest tailors. Those who knew him well might have wondered at the unusual haste with which the habitually languid Corinthian took the steps, his demeanor that of a man completely in control. No one would guess that in spirit, he was a man preparing to attend his own hanging, and eager to be done with it.

He handed his hat and gloves to his butler and asked as if the question were of no particular importance, "Where is Lady Valerie, Baldwin?"

Baldwin answered in tones that conveyed the depth of his sympathy, "In the library, Your Lordship." He cleared his throat delicately. "I believe she wishes a word with you, Your Lordship."

"The devil you say!" After the terrible scrape that Valerie had put herself in, he'd expected her to want nothing less than a chat with her older brother. What the deuce had come over his little sister? Usually sensible and biddable—the very best of young ladies—she had changed overnight into a rebellious termagant. And she had stubbornly remained so for the past two months.

He headed toward the library with long, effortless strides. Surely she had spent her rage in the hours-long tantrum she had thrown when he'd stopped her from utterly disgracing herself in the wee hours of this very morning.

The footman on duty at the library threw open the door as Moreland approached. Entering the huge book-lined room, he was met by his younger sister, Lady Valerie Forsythe.

Far from retiring in maidenly confusion, she spilled books from her lap and ran at him from the chair in which she had been seated, silken skirts rustling with the speed of her—Moreland could only think of one word—*attack*.

"How could you, Edward!" She formed her dainty hand into a fist and shook it violently under her brother's nose. "How *could* you?"

"I could . . . and did," Moreland said in a carefully bored drawl, "my dear Valerie, for the sake of your good name and for the honor of my house."

Lady Valerie flung around until her back was turned insultingly to her brother. How could he be such a blockhead! She had loved Harry Lytton since she was a child. How had her usually so perceptive brother missed it? And how could he now fail to realize that she'd turned to Giles Canderfield out of spite and in anguish?

Why didn't he ask her? Then she could dissolve in tears all over him and tell him how Harry'd said he'd never marry because he was a cripple. Maybe then Edward could do something to help. As it was, she daren't even let him see her face.

Her brother spoke to her as if she still faced him. "Did you really think such behavior would be countenanced?"

Angry because he didn't understand what she'd never tell him, she lashed out at him. "I *wanted* to go to Gretna Green with him. I *wanted* to marry Giles, and now you have ruined everything! I *hate* you!"

"You may hate me all you please, Valerie, but when you wed, it will be properly, as befits a member of this family, not over the anvil." His face was implacable. "You shall also be required to choose your husband from among the unexceptionable suitors of your acquaintance. I do not count Lieutenant Canderfeld among them."

"But he is so handsome!"

"Not a recommendation." Edward's tone was dry. "Lieutenant Canderfeld is a gazetted fortune hunter. His gambling debts are almost as large as your dowry."

"When you are in love, such things simply do not matter, Edward." She spoke in a world-weary voice, as if she were a woman of vast experience instead of a girl fresh from the schoolroom.

Edward made the mistake of letting his amusement show.

"How dare you." Valerie had caught the faint chuckle he had failed to repress. "How *dare* you!" She whirled to face him, her pretty face full of rage. "Surely I have decided on Giles in exactly the way I am expected to choose my mate! He is handsome and he is *whole*. What more do you want of me?"

She made the question merely rhetorical as she continued to rage without pause. "How could *you* understand? You are nothing but a dried-up old bachelor with no regard for anything but your work for the War Office. You are insensible to the finer feelings others are prey to."

Alarm rose in Moreland. "Valerie! You are never to mention my work again!" He spoke sharply, crushingly. The chit could ruin his effectiveness with her irresponsible remarks if she didn't learn to guard her tongue!

Valerie had the grace to look momentarily nonplussed. "I do know better than that, Edward. Forgive me. I shan't ever slip like that again." She moved close, the quicksilver of her mood changing, and gave him a contrite little hug. "Truly."

Moreland was frequently driven to distraction by her recent shifts in temperament, but he was not proof against her. He never had been since the moment shortly after his seventeenth birthday that she had come into the world. He patted her shoulder after he had returned her hug. "It's not a matter of life and death, Val."

"No, not this time. But there have been times when such a slip might have been."

Moreland was thunderstruck! How could she have known?

"Don't look so surprised," she told him, exasperated. "Your extra instructions to the solicitor, to the servants—your care to see that Aunt Marian came to visit—all these things clearly told me certain of your absences were not without danger."

"Dear God," he said weakly.

Valerie couldn't help it. After all, she was back on good terms with her dear Edward, and, so far, at very little cost to her comfort. "Yes," she said with a teasing glance, "He is, is He not?"

But Edward didn't respond to her playfulness. He was too occupied with worrying whether his surprisingly perceptive Valerie would guess his ulterior motive for taking her to the coast.

Chapter 2

Lady Rosalind, Countess Winston stood on the curb in front of the Ledbetters' ugly, expensive house waiting for the hackney cab one of the footmen had offered to hail for her. Now that the confrontation with her former employer was over, her heart was heavy. As long as she had been in the midst of a battle for her reputation, the seriousness of her dilemma had been held at bay. Now that her battle flags were no longer flying, she was cruelly aware of the position in which she found herself.

Where would she go? She was too proud to turn up on the doorstep of one of her friends from happier times. Asking for references to be written had been hard enough. Their kindness in the face of her threadbare necessity would be unbearable.

And Findlay had had a terrible time finding her employment as it was. Her beauty worked against her.

She could never go home. *Would* never go home!

Her father, the Earl of Summerfield, had left her no latitude when he had disowned her in a fit of rage upon her marriage to Hermes.

She herself had made matters worse between them by smilingly suggesting that her father was only angry because Hermes was a mere junior officer. General Lord Summerfield had taken deep offense at her gentle teasing. It had been too close to the mark.

Her marriage—bad enough that they had gone behind his back with a special license—had forced him to accept a penniless young officer, noble or no, as his son-in-law. Worse yet, he'd had to explain this unacceptable *fait accompli* to his very good friend General Bitwell.

Bitwell had been only waiting for the beautiful Lady Rosalind to grow up to declare his suit, never mind that he was nearly three times her age. Rosalind's father strongly suspected there was a very good chance that she had contracted marriage with the son of his neighbor just to avoid obliging him in the matter of his friend General Bitwell's attentions.

The Earl, in pique and embarrassment, had ordered his only child out of his house . . . and out of his life.

It had been a terrible moment for both of them. There was no way Rosalind would turn to him in her present distress.

"Thank you, Stubbs." She smiled at the footman as he handed her into the hackney. "You are very kind."

Stubbs's expression was a mixture of melancholy and compassion. "There's them that'll sore miss you, Miz Winston." He closed the door and stepped back before he could see the quick tears his kind remark had brought to her eyes.

She had not experienced a great deal of kindness in the Ledbetter home. This expression of his was nearly her undoing.

The cabbie cracked his whip halfheartedly, and the hackney rolled off, bearing the almost penniless Rosalind to an uncertain future.

Moreland had spent the better part of the last evening and night trying to come up with a solution to his dilemma. Or to be more honest, dilemmas, plural. For he had certainly spent enough time pacing the floor last night worrying about Valerie to classify her as a dilemma, too.

Blast the chit! Where had she gotten, in the two brief months since her come-out, this streak of rebellion that took her from one escapade to another with such wild disregard for her ancient name? And her own reputation, dammit! This latest folly could have been her undoing.

If Baldwin hadn't gotten wind of it from the silly goose's abigail . . . It didn't bear thinking on! He still paled when he considered the near thing it had been. Even now he repressed a shudder.

He gave himself a mental shake. His first duty now was to the matter at hand for Attleborough. How the blazes was he to establish a base of operations on the coast without arousing all sorts of suspicion—suspicion that would negate any chance he had of accomplishing his mission for King and Country.

With these two weighty concerns on his mind,

the Viscount had passed a fitful night and had awakened in a mood that put his whole staff on tiptoe. Baldwin, his peerless butler, learned of his employer's unhappy frame of mind when Lord Moreland had all but thrown Gates, his valet, bodily from his bedchamber. If His Lordship was in a pet that included even the giant Gates, his valet and boyhood companion, then things were at a pretty pass, indeed! Therefore, he intended to serve His Lordship breakfast himself. Baldwin obviously felt this was no time to leave his employer in the hands of a mere footman.

Moreland, presented with his morning newspaper, sent Baldwin to the buffet to choose what might tempt him to break his fast. While he waited, he sipped his coffee and perused the *Morning Post*.

Suddenly an announcement caught his eye. "Offered to the discriminating gentleman for a quiet retreat on the sea, Castle Winston, complete with a well-trained staff." There was more, but he didn't bother to read it.

Moreland slammed his Limoges cup down so quickly that Baldwin feared he'd cracked its saucer. The butler moved swiftly to mop up the slopped coffee and was happy to see His Lordship's great-grandmother's china still intact.

Moreland grinned up at him. "Baldwin." His voice had the lilt of a youth's. "Congratulate me for the luckiest devil you know and send for my writing things. I have a castle to lease!"

"Ah. How clever of Your Lordship. A time in the country is just the thing. Rather like a young gentleman going away on a repairing lease."

The Viscount looked at him blankly for an instant, then the butler's meaning penetrated. Of course! God bless Baldwin!

The solution to his second dilemma was suddenly obvious. It also gave him a reason for leaving town and taking up residence on the coast. Young Lady Valerie Forsythe was going on a female repairing lease. She was going to the seaside until any scandal that might have attached to her latest attempt to ruin herself had died away.

"Baldwin. What do I pay you?"

Baldwin quoted a generous sum with calm pride.

"Well, I have just decided to pay you half that again."

"Your Lordship!" Baldwin served his now hungry master his breakfast, then left the room in a state that bordered on euphoria to go fetch His Lordship's portable writing desk.

"Indeed, oh, indeed you are not imposing! In fact you are most, most welcome!" Andromeda knew she was babbling, but she didn't care. All she cared about was that they had Rosalind with them. Dear Rosalind, whose wondering letters had been their last link with their beloved brother, Hermes. Rosalind, about whom they had all been concerned.

And then the thought came like a lightning bolt—*Rosalind, who perfectly filled Andromeda's own need for one older person!* Andromeda could have hugged the beautiful woman until she cried for mercy! "You would be most welcome at any time, but you are *especially* welcome just now. Oh, how fortuitous!" Andromeda Winston was beside herself with gratitude for this further proof of God's kindness!

Perseus, standing quietly behind his twin sister until now, stepped forward. "Permit me to take your cloak and add my welcome to Andy's." He quickly removed the rain-sodden cloak from Rosalind's tired shoulders.

"Thank you." Her voice was low and musical, and Perseus heard the weariness that edged it.

He offered her his free arm. "Come into the morning room. It's coziest, and there's a good fire there." He shot her a blazingly beautiful smile. "Just ignore Andy until she comes out of alt. I'll take your cloak to the kitchen to dry and see if I can scare up some tea."

Rosalind, a bit bewildered by her young sister-in-law's effusive greeting, smiled at him gratefully and went with him into the morning room. They were accompanied by an Andromeda who seemed about to burst with excitement.

Perseus lead her across a pleasant room with large windows making up the far wall. Solicitously he seated her close beside the fire in a large wing chair and left to get their tea.

Andromeda took an identical chair opposite her, and studied her sister-in-law's lovely face. "You must be exhausted! We shall put you to bed the moment you have had your tea." She beamed at Rosalind, her smile as beautiful as her brother's.

"That is not necessary, really," Rosalind murmured as she held her hand out to the fire. "I will recover nicely the moment I am warm and fed."

"Of course," Andy said approvingly. "You are a soldier's wife and have followed the drum. You must be used to all sorts of hardships."

Rosalind looked into the sparkling eyes and

smiled. "Yes," she said simply. "It's a difficult life, but it would have been worse to have been left behind." Some of the shadows left her lovely gray eyes as she added, "Though it was not always easy to accompany your brother, I would not have missed it for the world."

Andromeda's cheerful voice interrupted her reminiscences. "I am so glad at last to see you again. We were all so young before you married and left, we scarce knew you. Now we all feel we know you well from the wonderful letters you wrote us while you were with Hermes." The girl blinked quickly and hurried on. "All of us were so disappointed when you did not stop to see us after . . . after . . ."

"I was sorry that I had to go straight to my job as governess." Rosalind's low voice was husky. "After sending you Hermes's charger, there were no funds, you see." She smiled gently to take any sting out of her words. "Junior officers are not particularly well paid, you know."

Perseus's arrival with their tea interrupted them. "Here we are! Just buttered bread, but the tea is hot and should help." He set the heavy silver waiter on the small table beside Andromeda and pulled a chair near for himself.

"Cassiopeia will join us shortly. And I've no doubt the other twins, Castor and Pollux, will be here in a flash. They always seem to be on the alert for tea." He added, as an enthusiastic afterthought, "I say! Isn't it jolly not to have to explain that we're all named after stellar constellations?"

He and Andromeda were in agreement on that, Rosalind could see at once.

Andromeda said softly as she poured, "Except of course Hermes. Being firstborn, he could only be messenger from the gods."

Perseus leaned back in his chair and said with understandable force, "God protect the unwary from fathers who are Greek scholars!"

"And amateur astronomers, as well. From such, heaven defend us," Andromeda added fervently.

Rosalind had barely accepted her cup from Andromeda when the morning room door slammed open to admit two boys of about nine years of age. They stormed into the room like a little whirlwind and threw themselves down on the hearth rug at her feet.

"You're our sister . . ." one began, propping his chin on his hands.

". . . Rosalind. Hermes's wife," the other said, smiling up at her as he unconsciously copied his twin's posture. Then together they finished in a breathless rush, "Aren't you?"

"Well, yes, I am." Rosalind had almost never seen the twins and certainly could not find a thing by which to tell the boys apart. To her unaccustomed eye, they were as alike as two peas in a pod. What marvelous games that must allow them to play! She chuckled to herself at the thought of it.

They'd been much younger while Hermes had lived, so she'd had no word of any escapades. Somehow she was certain that if she were to receive a letter from Castle Winston now, she would have word of many!

Rosalind wished she had continued the copious correspondence she had initiated with the family while on the Continent. It would have made her present situation so much easier. But mail was always slow to catch up with the army, and so many letters went astray that, to her sorrow, she hadn't known they'd enjoyed and answered her lengthy missives.

As if he'd read her mind, Perseus asked quietly, "Why did you not keep writing? We all missed your letters, you know."

"Ah, did you?" Rosalind's voice was sad. "I wish I had known." She'd had a family and not known it. Suddenly she had to fight tears for all the long, lonely months that she'd thought of them. . . . "I would have kept up." She smiled and her smile dazzled them. "But there was so little of interest to write about once I had begun my employment with Mrs. Ledbetter." Spreading her hands toward them, she made a helpless little gesture. "Nothing you would have enjoyed hearing at any rate," she finished ruefully.

"Was it that bad?" Andy asked quietly.

"Oh, dear. Was I whining? I *do* apologize!"

"Good heavens. What for? It would *have* to be dreadful, being a governess for anybody with a name so obviously cit as Ledbetter." Andy was all sympathy.

"Cits pay the best," Rosalind said dryly.

"That's certainly a consideration," Perseus said with a deep sigh.

"Truly!" Andromeda's comment was heartfelt. Then she brightened. "But that does bring us neatly to the subject at hand!"

"What subject at hand, henwit?" Perseus had been polite long enough. He wasn't going to coun-

tenance another of Andromeda's harebrained starts
with his sister-in-law drooping with fatigue.

"The subject of this wonderful example of God's
grace in bringing us Rosalind just at this time."

"What *are* you talking about, Andy?" Perseus
glowered.

"How can you call me the henwit, when it's
obvious that you're the one with the attic to let?"

Perseus bristled. "There is nothing wrong with
my brainbox, sister dear."

"No, darling twin," she said as if he were anything but. "It's your lamentable memory that is at
fault."

The Gemini twins, Castor and Pollux, looked
from one to the other with a great deal of interest.

Rosalind wondered where this odd conversation
was going.

"My memory is fine, thank you."

"Not if you don't recall your comment from the
cliffside rose garden, it isn't."

Perseus's fine brow wrinkled in concentration.
"What comment?" he said finally, obviously reluctant to ask.

"The one in which you said," Andromeda drew it
out, relishing her small triumph. " 'You're going to
need at least one person who is older, and how are
you going to manage that?' " She looked at him in a
decidedly superior way. "And now it is all taken
care of, my doubting friend!"

"What in blazes do you mean, Andy?" He
scowled at her. "You can't mean to saddle Rosalind
with our problems!"

"Oh, but I do. Indeed I do. We *need* Rosalind, and

she needs us, and it will all work out splendidly! Will it not, Rosalind?"

Rosalind couldn't think of a suitable comment. She wasn't even sure she understood what the older twins were talking about. They knew she needed them, and they needed *her* for something. It didn't even matter to her what they needed her for. Their need was like healing balm to her lacerated spirit.

She didn't care a whit what she was agreeing to. Not one whit. Without the slightest hesitation, she nodded her head and answered, "Yes."

Chapter 3

Rosalind settled in at Castle Winston as if she had been there all her life. It was true that the area was one familiar to her. She had grown up, pampered and guarded, on the immense property that bounded that of Castle Winston, with the very same thunderous sea in her ears.

The emotionally austere home of her soldier father was a far cry from the loving, quarreling warmth of her present abode, however, and she was becoming aware of the source of her late husband's quiet happiness more and more every day.

Severely repressing feelings of disloyalty to the lonely man who had raised her in utter luxury and terrifying loneliness, Rosalind permitted herself to enjoy the company of her late husband's boisterous siblings. After three years alone, she was deeply grateful for the support of her family by marriage.

Rosalind was looking out the morning room

window into the rose garden when Andromeda came whooping into the room. "Look! Look! It has come!"

She stopped next to Rosalind in a flurry of skirts. Thrusting a sheet of heavy vellum embossed with a noble seal under Rosalind's nose, she crowed, "Is it not wonderful? My notice—the notice I placed in the *Morning Post*—was successful!"

Rosalind took the letters from the excited girl and removed it from the close proximity of her own nose, the better to see it. Scanning it hastily while Andy danced from foot to foot and explained about the notice, she said into her sister-in-law's first pause for breath, "Andy, from this I gather you have leased the castle to"—she looked again at the bold signature that was splashed across the bottom of the crisp page—"someone named Moreland."

"Yes, yes. Oh, yes. Is it not splendid?"

Rosalind was slow to answer.

Andromeda gave her a quick hug and a little shake. "Oh, do be glad, Rosalind. We've talked about this. It is an answer to our prayers. Do be glad."

"Yes, of course, dear. I am glad for you."

"You don't sound particularly glad," Andy accused.

"It is not that I'm not glad, dear. It is just that now that it is upon us, I am worried about how we will pull it off." In truth, she had no idea how they were going to accomplish Andy's wild scheme. Somehow she'd thought that they would just rub along on what Perseus had made from his brief foray into smuggling—a dangerous and illegal activity she had every intention of seeing he never engaged in again—now that spring was here and the garden about to show them some encouragement.

"We shall. And it will be a marvelous lark, too. You will see."

Rosalind smiled at her dear friend's enthusiasm and fervently hoped so!

Valerie threw her brother another fulminating glare and clutched at the strap on her side of the luxurious traveling coach. "I cannot believe you are doing this to me. To me, your own dear little sister!" She spoke as if Lytton were not even in the carriage but *they* were still raging at each other in the privacy of their library.

"If you were, my own dear little sister, obedient and properly behaved, this would not be happening to you. You, however, and not I, have done this to yourself with your irresponsible actions." Moreland's face was stern.

"How can you call falling in love irresponsible?"

"Believe me," her brother said in a cool voice, "the way you fall in love, I find it quite simple."

Valerie turned a shoulder, her pretty mouth in a pout. Moreland ignored her.

Just as the atmosphere in the coach was becoming unbearable, Valerie burst out, "I cannot understand this. It is just too dreadful to be away from home and to have to put up with strange servants, as well. I need my very own abigail, not some cow-handed country bumpkin!"

"Do not use cant," Moreland corrected automatically. "I'm certain the maid provided will be fine. As we will not be frequently in society, I am certain she will suffice."

He frowned. "You may count yourself fortunate, by the way, that I did not sack your abigail. The next time you involve her in one of your scrapes, be assured I will."

"You are hateful!" She looked at him accusingly. "You are bringing Gates for yourself."

"That is because the castle is not at present equipped with a valet. Lord Winston's valet left when the old gentleman died." Moreland strove to hide his own satisfaction at this state of affairs. He was certain no one could serve him as well as Gates. He smiled to think of the ways in which Gates served him. Valet, confidant, friend in shared peril—Gates had been all of these.

In fact, his thoughts drifted, Gates had been with him the night he had seen *her*. Auburn hair catching lights from the campfire, grace to rival a naiad, and quiet courage in her beautiful face, she had bent to her task over the fire and done it in spite of the occasional enemy shot that crackled in the night.

He had crouched in the filth and rags that made up his disguise by that very campfire. Close enough to touch her. Close enough to ask her name, close enough . . .

But of course he could not. He was under orders. Besides, she was a mere soldier's woman—for he had seen no ring on that beautifully shaped hand—and he was a nobleman with responsibilities to his family.

That moment by that campfire was one he had never shared with Gates.

". . . And she will probably pull my hair!"

Moreland became aware of his sister again in time to hear her complaint. He sent his friend

Lytton an exasperated look. "Don't be a peagoose. Of course she won't pull your hair."

"But just think! I have never done anyone's hair except my own and yours, Andy. Suppose I pull her hair?"

Cassiopeia's wail brought a grimace from Perseus. "Stow it, Cassie. Do you think I've the slightest idea how to be a butler? You'll just have to do your best, just like the rest of us."

Andromeda looked at him in grateful amazement. Hadn't he, until this very moment, been the most opposed to and critical of her plan to keep things going at the castle? She threw him an affectionate smile.

"Don't get all sticky on me, Andy," he muttered.

Much encouraged by her twin's cooperative attitude she continued her instructions. "We have Jim and Frank Green from the village to act as footmen. Their mother agreed to accept vegetables and wine for their pay for the summer."

"Lucky for you the old harridan has a taste for spirits, or the boys would have gone to help with the farming somewhere, and you'd have been out of luck." Perseus was reluctantly impressed with his sister's inventiveness in procuring footmen for her scheme.

"Lucky for me I have a brother who smuggled spirits."

"Ssshhhh!" Castor and Pollux both hushed her, looking furtively around. They had been schooled never to mention their brother's recent effort to earn enough money to keep the castle running and food on their plates. Never. Ever.

"Thank you, twins." Perseus ruffled the hair of the nearest.

Pollux looked up with a grin, grateful for his adored brother's notice.

"Now we come to the Gemini." Andromeda looked at them affectionately. "It would be better if you were not twins, I think. If Viscount Moreland should ever chance to mention twins to any of our neighbors, the fat will surely be in the fire."

The twins' faces were identical wary masks.

Andromeda took a deep breath and plunged in. "So one of you is going to be the scullery maid." There, she'd said it!

The twins exploded from their spot on the floor as one being. "No!" they howled in unison as they ran for the door.

"Damn!" Perseus was off in hot pursuit.

Rosalind spoke from in front of the looking glass where she was busy blackening Cassiopeia's fine golden brows with charcoal, "Do you think this will work, Andromeda?"

Andromeda replied heatedly, "Of course it will work. It must work. There is simply nothing else to be done unless we are all to starve." She made a little gesture meant to apologize for speaking to Rosalind so, then continued earnestly. "What we make leasing the castle to Moreland will keep us through the winter and help improve the farmland as Perseus has planned. When the farms are producing again, we will no longer be in such dire straits. Until then we cannot use any of the money to keep us somewhere else. We just have to pass successfully as the castle servants. We must." With that impassioned speech, Andromeda plopped into the nearest chair and burst into tears.

"Oh, dearest." Rosalind flew to her side. "You must not cry. Your plan is an excellent one. Of course we will succeed."

"But you doubted we would."

"Never!"

"But you asked if I thought it would work. . . ." Andy was bewildered.

For an instant Rosalind was puzzled. Then she understood. "Oh, Andy! I meant the charcoal on Cassie's eyebrows." Both young women dissolved in laughter.

Perseus appeared at that moment, a struggling twin under either arm. "I'm glad somebody finds something to laugh about in this situation!" He shook the twins briefly and set them upon their feet. "Tell her."

The twins glared at their, until this moment, adored older brother.

Perseus glared back.

Castor was the first to speak. "We have agreed . . ."

". . . to do as you ask . . ." Pollux added.

". . . if we can . . ." Castor continued.

". . . do it the way Perseus says we can," they finished in unison, their faces a mixture of triumph and stubbornness.

"What"—Andromeda was wary—"did Perseus say you might do?" She gave her own twin an ominous look.

"He said we could take turns being the scullery maid."

Andromeda sighed with relief. "Very well. That should not pose any problem."

Until, Rosalind thought, *someone gives the twin playing the role of page an order that the next twin fails to carry out when they switch places.* Suddenly Rosalind wasn't so sure Andromeda's plan would work after all.

Chapter 4

"Remember to keep your eyes down," Rosalind cautioned as she carefully scrutinized the young Winstons lined up for her inspection. She smoothed the worn lapel of Perseus's "butler disguise," as he called it, and went on. "Not one of you has the look of a servant. You will just have to avoid showing your faces until the Viscount and his party get used to you."

She fluffed the ruffles of Cassie's cap, checked to see that her charcoal-darkened eyebrows had not been smeared, and told her, "You are lovely, Cassie, even in that dreadful cap. Dark eyebrows with your blue eyes give you the look of an Irish Colleen."

Cassiopeia smiled a bit more bravely and teasingly dropped Rosalind a lovely curtsy.

Rosalind nearly fainted. "Oh, dear! Oh, my, no!"

Every eye turned on her. Perseus asked sharply, "What is it, Roz? What's the matter?"

Rosalind sank down on the marble bench beside

the impressive steps leading to front door. Her posture was one of dejection as she studied them, chin on hand.

Andromeda stepped forward and laid a hand on her shoulder. "Are you all right, dear?"

"Yes. I am fine." She straightened with determination. "I simply feel like a ninny."

"Why?" three voices asked in chorus. The Gemini twins, silent for once, just watched, awestruck.

"Curtsies. When Cassie curtsied, I knew we were deeply in trouble. And, of course, it is all my fault!"

Andromeda said, slowly, not understanding, "Cassie curtsies beautifully."

Perseus smacked his fist into the palm of his other hand, "Of course. That's the problem, isn't it?" He began to grin.

"Exactly." Rosalind smiled apologetically. "When Cassie swept me a curtsy that would have been admired at court, I realized she could never do that as a servant. Servants don't really curtsy. They . . . They sort of . . ."

"Bob!" Perseus exclaimed as his mind discovered the perfect word to describe the quick dip female servants offered their employers.

"Who? Bob?" Castor queried. Then his pleasantly inquiring expression turned truculent. "I wanted to be called John, not Bob. You promised." He glared at Perseus.

Pollux was equally disconcerted. He added earnestly, both by way of reminder and in aid of his twin, "That was the only way you got Castor and me to agree to be the page and the scullery maid. By giving us a good old everyday name for when we're the page."

"Especially after saying you were going to call us *Polly* . . ." Castor whined the word with sarcastic emphasis.

". . . when we were being the scullery maid." Pollux began to look decidedly uncooperative in his turn. "You *promised* we could be John when we are the page."

Together they said, "John, not Bob."

"Oh, do hush, Gemini!" Andromeda lost patience with the boys. "We're worrying about another problem entirely."

"Look . . ." Perseus, struggling with concealed laughter, tried for a calmer tone. "It's very simple, really. You three girls"—he looked from Andy and Cassie to Rosalind—"will just have to forget all those long hours of being taught to do it properly, and just think of a curtsy like a hiccup."

All three young ladies stared.

"You know," he persisted. "Just jig down and bob up again like a hiccup. That will fill the bill admirably."

Rosalind looked at him very seriously and tried to follow his advice. The result was still far too graceful. She tried again immediately with better results.

Andromeda, not wishing to come behind in any good thing, solemnly dipped and straightened quickly. She grinned as Perseus nodded approval.

Cassie, over her momentary hurt at having caused such a furor with her lovely curtsy, tried to do as the other two did, muttering, "Hic-up, hic-up," to herself to get the proper rhythm. She burst into a radiant smile. "Perseus! You are exactly right. It *is* a hiccup."

Walking from one to the other, his head cocked judiciously to one side, Perseus gave such serious advice that the younger twins could bear it no longer. They dropped to the ground and began to roll around on the newly green lawn in gales of laughter that sent them all off.

"Cease!" Suddenly a voice like an icy wind cut at them. "You will stop this highly unseemly behavior at once! Desist rolling around on that damp grass like village idiots. I never! Furthermore, I demand an explanation of this tasteless charade this very minute!"

Rosalind whipped around toward the sound of the voice and stared. A tiny apparition in a long black cloak shook a slender cane at the assembled Winstons. Quivering with indignation, the diminutive lady added, "You will all march inside and get out of those ridiculous outfits. Now! March!"

The lawn was cleared of Winstons in the space of a single heartbeat, and Rosalind was left alone to face the fierce little old lady in the faded cloak.

"And just who might you be, young woman?" The dragon lifted her head and peered haughtily down her nose at Rosalind.

Rosalind never for a moment considered telling her she was "Mrs. Rose, the Housekeeper" as they had all decided she should be. Without a moment's hesitation she answered honestly. "I am Rosalind Winston, Hermes's relict. Am I so greatly changed?"

"Bless my soul. Of course, of course. My dear, my dear." The ice was gone as quickly as if the little tyrant had experienced her own personal Spring thaw. "Now you are dear Hermes's widow. You were only a child the last time I saw you. How glad

I am to see you again!" She came close and offered
Rosalind her dry cheek.

Unhesitatingly Rosalind kissed her, and the birdlike woman, taking her arm to lean upon, steered
Rosalind into the house.

Perseus went to search out something for tea. He
claimed he was just settling into his assigned role of
butler. The other Winstons claimed he was running
off to play least in sight while their former nanny
tore a strip off each of them in turn.

Appearing with his tray a quarter of an hour
later, Perseus found his siblings with whole skins.
Miss Leticia Evans, spinster daughter of the late
vicar of Palesworthy, and former tyrant of nursery
and schoolroom at Castle Winston, was seated by
the fire in the morning room in serious conversation
with Rosalind and Andromeda.

"I shall come and help, of course," she said
firmly. Ignoring the gratitude of the assembled
company, she told them, "And I shall convince the
Freeps, Cook and Tom Coachman, that they cannot
want to miss the fun as well. I suspect they are a bit
bored with being pensioned off, as both of them are
getting quite chubby. What have you done about
footmen?"

Andromeda told her of her arrangement for
footmen with some pride.

"Excellent! Smart girl. Good wine will be better
for Elsie Green than that blue ruin she gets at the
pub, and she *will* drink. Her bad habit might as well
do *you* some good. Housemaids?"

Andromeda shifted uncomfortably, not quite sure
she would gain her former nanny's approval with

her reply. "We thought we would just do as we have done lately. All of us have been sharing the housekeeping duties."

Andromeda's instinct had been right. Nanny Evans asked sweetly, "Is *that* why the floor in the great hall looks as if the Royal Hussars had camped there? I *had* wondered!"

Her next words were spoken with some asperity. "No, it won't do. Go back and make the same arrangements with Elsie Green—vegetables and wine—for the sisters. Get the oldest and third oldest," she ordered. "Second oldest—who is it, Maggie?—looks to me as if she's going to follow in her mother's footsteps. Saw her tipsy Saturday evening."

She put a frail hand to her forehead and pursed her lips, deep in thought. Looking up, she demanded. "How many will that make?"

Andromeda, self-styled spokesman for the group, said, "Housekeeper, cook, and coachman"— she beamed at her former nanny, giving her full credit for the last two—"butler, lady's maid, chambermaid—that's me—page and scullery maid, two footmen, and two housemaids. That makes twelve! Rather a respectable staff, don't you think?"

Nanny Evans gave an offended sniff. "For Castle Winston it is pitiful! And you forgot me. I must serve in some capacity. I do not intend to miss the fun, even if I do make thirteen!"

Rosalind hoped that the number thirteen did not, as many dinner hostesses believed, make for bad luck.

"You must choose your own work, then, for I am

quite thought out." Andromeda was pleased with the arrangements she had made in spite of Nanny Evans's lack of enthusiasm.

"Perhaps I should relinquish my position as housekeeper to you and become a chambermaid with Andromeda," Rosalind offered.

"No." Miss Evans refused the idea. "I shall—"

"They're here! Hurry. Hurry! Run, they are coming up the long stretch over the cliffs this very minute!" One of the Gemini screeched breathlessly as he pounded into the room.

Rosalind jumped to her feet, "Quickly, Perseus, to the door. We shall meet them, you and I. The rest of you line up in the hall! Castor—or is it Pollux?— run and get Jim and Frank from the kitchen. We must have footmen. Run!"

As the boy tore out of the room, Andromeda bumped into Rosalind, then turned back to assist Nanny Evans from her chair. Rosalind ran for the front door, colliding with Cassiopeia in the hall.

"Where shall we stand, Rosalind?" Cassie's eyes filled her face.

Rosalind sketched a line as she hurried past, "Along there, get everybody together. See that they look right, Andy," she called over her shoulder as she ran out the door.

Perseus stuck his head back in. "We'll stall them as long as we can!"

Rosalind took up a place beside Perseus on the broad front steps. They could just hear the jingle of harness. Soon Viscount Moreland and his entourage would be upon them, and all she could think was that she wished they were going to be more—or fewer—than *thirteen* in number.

Chapter 5

"There it is, Valerie. A handsome pile you will agree." Lytton pulled his wind-tousled head back into the carriage to smile at her.

Lady Valerie gave him an enigmatic stare and vouchsafed no response.

Moreland, looking at it as they approached, had to admit he was impressed with Castle Winston. It sprawled as well as towered, clinging to the headland, dispensing the usual loom of such edifices, in proportions that were pleasing to his eye.

The mellow stones were weathered pale, and the whole effect was somehow lighter than he'd expected. Lighter in more than appearance, as some one of its owners had caused large windows to be cut through the thick walls at intervals frequent enough to provide considerable light to the interior as well.

Valerie, for her part, finally sniffed.

Lytton settled back in his place, his effort to cheer the sulking girl seeming to have exhausted him.

Moreland, suppressing a sigh at the thought of a summer spent in the company of these two, continued his inspection of the castle. Finishing his perusal of the parapets, he turned his attention to the two figures waiting on the steps. The butler seemed rather young—he'd demand an explanation for that later. The housekeeper, standing straight and obviously nervous in her sober black gown with the many-keyed chatelaine hanging against its skirt, was certainly not of an age approaching retirement, either.

The driver stopped their conveyance with a flourish, directly in front of the steps. Moreland frowned as he assisted Valerie from the mud-spattered coach. He hoped this staff, forced on him by the terms of the lease, were going to be able to make his stay comfortable.

It was not that he was unduly concerned about his own needs. He's spent too many nights sleeping in muddy ditches behind enemy lines to be particular, and was sure Lytton felt the same. He just didn't want Valerie to have cause to kick up a dust. Accustomed to the precise order and sumptuous comfort of their home in Town, she might make unfortunate comparisons.

"Milord, welcome to Castle Winston." The young butler bowed with too much grace and gestured toward the woman beside him. "The housekeeper, Mrs. Rose."

"Mrs. Rose" curtsied briefly.

Moreland gave the butler their own names and escorted Valerie into the house.

Remembering Miss Evans's comment about the great hall, Perseus rushed to introduce the others. "Your staff, milord."

Moreland saw the tops of two mobcaps—their wearers too shy or too disinterested to look up at him—two large, rather raw-boned footmen who looked distinctly uncomfortable in their green, gold-laced livery, and a pair of children regarding him solemnly from eyes that were disconcertingly similar, who were obviously the page or provision boy and the scullery maid.

There was one other creature who refused to meet his gaze. She was a willowy girl whose face he was unable to see, as well. He took her to be the lady's maid he had been promised for his sister.

Wondering if the owners of the castle suffered from some severe mental derangement that left them unable to look upon the face of a servant, he directed his comment to the top of this one's head. "My sister is tired from her journey. Would you kindly show her to her room?"

Perseus tried not to glance at the beautiful blonde beside Moreland. He couldn't afford to have his senses jangled. Keeping his face wooden, he said, "Cassie, see to your mistress."

It was fortunate Andromeda had just warned them to keep their heads down. Even so, Perseus saw the sudden quiver of ruffles on Cassiopeia's mobcap as her sensibilities jolted at the word *mistress*. In spite of her shock, however, she managed a stumbling curtsy as she led Valerie toward the stairs.

A frown passed briefly across the Viscount's face. Then he shook his head, resisting the impulse to run a hand across his forehead. No, he told himself. Surely he had not heard anyone say "hiccup"! It must be that he was more tired than he'd thought. And if he was, certainly Lytton was.

"Kindly show Lieutenant Lytton and myself to our rooms. We'd like dinner at six."

In the kitchen, Miss Evans was giving instruction in a hissing stream of whispered words that sounded like a teakettle on the hob. Rosalind and the Winstons were grouped around her, listening for all they were worth.

"Pay attention." She shook her cane. "That valet of his may be here at any moment. Oh, how much better it would be if only we could have found a way to exclude him!"

Rosalind exchanged a smile with Andromeda at hearing the "we" in her little speech. It was such a relief to have a fellow conspirator who knew all about life belowstairs.

Rosalind had to say, "Dear Miss Evans, it is such a wonderful thing that you have come to guide us through this maze we have all so heedlessly entered."

"Indeed!" Cassiopeia's eyes were round with the fright of a near disaster. "If my 'mistress'"—she glared at her brother—"hadn't told me to help her to bed for a nap and sent me away, I make certain that I would have put my foot in it already!" She left them.

"Not to worry!" the little lady in the chair by the fire assured them cheerily. "With me to tell you what to do, you will none of you put a foot wrong!"

To a man, those around her fervently hoped her confidence would be justified.

"There is the problem of dinner." Rosalind was reluctant to bring that hurdle up, but the afternoon was slipping away.

"Yes. If Cook doesn't arrive soon, we shall have to contrive." Nanny looked at Perseus. "What is there in the house to serve?"

"How on earth would I know?" Perseus looked like a horse that had just seen its first steam engine.

"Of course. I'm sorry. You are only playing at being the butler. Knowing dear Rosalind was newly come, I'd placed the burden of the pantry on you."

"Huh! Wouldn't be much of a burden. The cupboard is as bare as that of the old woman in the shoe!"

"This is no time for nursery rhymes, Lord Winston!" Miss Evans reprimanded him sharply. "Quickly. Go hitch up the pony cart. I'll make a list, and you can buy what's on it for dinner tonight and breakfast tomorrow. That will give us time to think."

"I had better go," Rosalind offered. "Perseus would be most missed. He's the butler, after all."

"Very well." Miss Evans looked toward the table in the center of the servants' hall, and some of the assurance went out of her. "Let's hope Cassiopeia can get those two boys ready to serve by the time you get back and we get dinner cooked!"

They all turned to follow her gaze. There was a collective sigh as they watched the farm boys in livery, their ruddy faces twisted in scowls of fierce concentration, trying to remember all that young Lady Cassiopeia was trying to teach them.

Rosalind took her cloak down from its peg,

returned to Miss Evans for the list, and left to find the pony cart with a heart full of foreboding for this, the Viscount Moreland's first dinner at Castle Winston.

Chapter 6

Rosalind returned from her errand to a gay scene in the kitchen. Boiling pots of water made cheery wreaths of steam above the cookstove, and there was a merry bustle as various Winstons ran to and fro fetching this bowl or that platter at the instruction of a round little tyrant with a long spoon in her hand. Cook had come.

Miss Evans bustled up. "Here, Lady Winston, let me take some of those."

Rosalind laughed. "Thank you. My bundles seem to be overflowing their basket." She took the basket to the huge scrubbed table where the cook met her.

"Thank heavens, child! We have the pots on the boil, and now that you are here with the provisions to put in 'em, I expect we shall be able to have dinner at six, after all." She laughed merrily, her eyes twinkling at Rosalind. "But it will be a near thing, milady, a near thing."

Rosalind slipped out of her cloak, and one of the

"footmen" took it, folded it over his arm as he so recently had been taught, and walked with measured tread to hang it on its peg.

Rosalind laughed with delight. How could she have been so blue-deviled on her journey to the village? With such wonderful conspirators, everything would simply have to turn out all right!

Cook quickly began plopping the various freshly washed contents of Rosalind's bundles into the pots. A shake of this here, a dash of that in another place, and soon the kitchen was filled with hearty aromas.

Andromeda said, "Look. Smell." She suited her actions to her commands and danced around the stove, wilting her curls as she sniffed at the steam rising from the large collection of pots. "Not only is disaster averted, but if one were to judge by the appreciative looks on the faces of the Gemini, culinary history is about to be made in this wonderful, long-neglected kitchen!"

Cook beamed, the younger twins scowled, and Rosalind and Andromeda gave each other quick, gleeful hugs, their spirits high with this success in the kitchen. Then the two young women moved with one accord to the stairs.

"There is a good chance we will be needed to put the table to rights," Andromeda informed her sister-in-law just as Rosalind said, "Do you think Perseus may need us to help?"

They smothered their laughter as they approached the green baize door that marked the end of the servants' part of the house, and Andromeda said with mock solemnity, "All must be perfect for the master of the castle and his guests."

Rosalind confirmed this with an enthusiastic nod that sent her mobcap forward over her eyes. She pushed it back into place, making a mental note to pin it firmly in the future.

The two of them arrived in the huge, formal dining room just in time to save Perseus's sanity. He stood with a stack of plates and a heap of silverware before him on the end of the thirty-foot-long table. On his face there was a look of such comic desperation that only a quick pinch from Rosalind kept Andromeda from bursting into laughter.

He looked up at them. "Don't you think, that after eating three meals a day all my life, I would know where the devil to put these damn things?" he asked them plaintively.

Rosalind forgave his profanity, knowing it merely indicated the depth of his frustration.

Andromeda started to scold, realized Rosalind had no doubt heard worse in army camps, and took pity on him instead. "Here, Pers," she said as they hurried to him. "We'll do it. You just watch and learn."

Within minutes the table was set for three. Rosalind decided to move the centerpiece nearer the head of the table so the guests could enjoy it at dinner. "This is lovely, Perseus."

He took the heavy silver epergne from her. "Yes. Flowers are one of the luxuries we've never had to do without, thanks to the three faithful old retainers who keep on tending them. They insist it keeps their rheumatism at bay to stay busy in spite of being retired. God knows we love 'em for it."

"I can imagine." She straightened a few blooms that had drooped awry in Perseus's swift moving of the epergne and looked up from her handiwork to smile at him.

Moreland entered the room at just that instant and was startled by the beauty the smile brought to her face.

The moment she saw him, Rosalind came to attention, her face suddenly grave again. "Good evening, Your Lordship!" She abbreviated her curtsy to something between its usual grace and the bob they had all three practiced on the front lawn.

He inclined his head graciously. "Good evening. Mrs. Rose, isn't it?"

"Yes, Your Lordship." She watched him a bit warily. What was he doing in the dining room without the rest of his party—and before dinner was announced?

As if he'd read her thoughts, he said, "I'm afraid I have no idea where to find the drawing room."

"Oh." She blushed at having been startled into the exclamation. "This way, please."

"Will you be so kind as to have footmen shepherd the rest of my party?" His gaze locked on her face, enjoying her heightened color.

"Of course, Your Lordship." She threw open the double doors to the withdrawing room and stood aside, slightly flustered by his perusal. She was annoyed at his boldness, too, knowing that if she stood before him as Rosalind, Countess Winston, his eyes would not linger so.

But she was a mere servant for the time being. Best she accustom herself to her role and give over her sensibilities from a former life.

Heartened by her decision, she brought herself back to her duty. One quick glance told her the drawing room was fine. It was well dusted and had a welcome warmth from the cheery fire one of the footmen had built while she was in the village. She made a mental note to praise him, and hoped they would all be as successful in keeping ahead of the Viscount and his sister and friend in the matter of having the rooms they might use clean before they blundered into them.

"Thank you, Mrs. Rose."

"Your Lordship." She was careful not to smile, and left him with a brisk rustle of skirts. So many things to try to remember! Had Mrs. Henderson, her father's housekeeper, smiled when her father dismissed her? She would have to find a quiet moment mentally to review the behavior of her father's small army of servants. Otherwise, someone who looked to her for guidance—and that could be any one of the masqueraders—could make a mistake that might give the game away. She felt the ruffles on her mobcap move as she shook her head, worrying about the pitfalls that lay in wait for "the staff" of Castle Winston.

"Ah, there you are, Moreland!" Lytton strode into the drawing room, his scarlet regimentals seeming to brighten it. "Never should have found you if there hadn't been a footman waiting outside my door."

Moreland smiled at his friend. "It is a little daunting. But a pleasant place, I think. The chimney draws in my bedchamber, and I take that as a mark of great luxury."

Lytton smiled. "Are you by any chance still remembering that smoke-filled hut where we nearly froze to death in—" He broke off as they heard footsteps in the hall.

Valerie, resplendent in a pale blue gown that would not have been out of place at the most fashionable table in Town, swept into the room. The footman who had led her from the upstairs hallway bowed himself out and closed the doors.

"You look lovely, Val." Her brother smiled fondly at her.

"Yes, indeed." Lytton made her a small bow, his gaze lingering.

Moreland couldn't resist. "Your hair is especially attractive tonight."

"Well"—Valerie took his bait—"she did pull it. Twice!" She locked gazes with her brother, then decided to be fair. "I think she was a bit nervous. She did do a nice job, however, so we are even."

"Even?" One of Moreland's dark eyebrows rose a fraction in inquiry.

"Yes. I said she'd pull my hair. You said she'd do a good job. Even." She turned to her brother's friend. "Is your room to your satisfaction, Lieutenant Lytton?" She looked at him intently.

"Quite." His color rose under her stare.

At that moment double doors at the far end of the room opened. The young butler announced in dignified tones, "Dinner is served," and fervently hoped that he was not remiss in failing to preface his announcement with a "Your Lordship." There was a lot to this butlering that he was woefully ignorant of.

Perseus seated the Viscount himself and watched to see the footmen do a commendable job with the other two.

All three of the "servants" were relieved to see the party take up their own napkins, shake them out of fold, and place them in their own laps. Perseus stifled a grin as he saw the thankful glances Jim and Frank Green shot heavenward. They'd been appalled when he'd told them to be on the alert for some sign that the guests expected them to perform this service for them.

Perseus suffered anxiety throughout the whole meal. He poured wine with a hand that he had to fight to keep from shaking, and watched like a hawk as Jim and Frank offered each dish to the diners.

With a feeling of desperation, he checked and rechecked the list Rosalind had written so that the proper things would be served at the proper times. Clinging to the little slip of paper half hidden on the sideboard, he progressed through his ordeal in orderly fashion.

He had to stifle firmly the urgent desire to snatch plates away before the people had finished eating what was on them so that he could get to the next thing on the list—and the next—and be done with it. He felt as if the meal were lasting a century!

He was almost reduced to gibbering when Frank, seeing the Lieutenant's arm gone, almost passed him by with the roast beef. At the last instant Frank saved himself, offered the meat he knew the young officer would never be able to cut up, and passed on with a silent sigh of relief when the Lieutenant quietly refused it.

When Moreland, Valerie, and Lytton had finished their meal, they returned, all three, to the drawing room. The men accompanied her in deference to her being alone. Their passage was slow and full of dignity.

The instant the "butler" had closed the dining room doors behind them, the three nervously perspiring "servants" rushed as one man out of the elegant chamber and down to the kitchen. Their passage was nothing short of a rout.

Chapter 7

"We must plan, Harry. God knows we must stop the bastard before he carries any more secrets to France."

Lytton's face was as grim as his friend's. Both had been waiting impatiently for Valerie to retire so that they could get to the business they had come to perform.

"Shall we try to find the study?" Moreland shrugged even as he suggested it.

"A desk would be helpful." Lytton laughed, adding, "And no doubt the exercise we will have in searching for the room in question will be beneficial."

Moreland smiled a twisted smile. "I could ring for a footman."

"What? And miss our adventure?"

"As you will." Moreland's smile became more natural, glad to see this upturn in his friend's spirits, and led the way down the nearest hall. The

first door he tried was the music room, attested to
by the pair of pianofortes and the harp they could
see by the light from the hallway. The room was
chilly and had a forlorn look. They went on to the
next set of double doors.

Row upon row of books filled a large, well-
appointed room. It, too, was cool, in spite of the fire
that burned in one of the two fireplaces cut into
opposing walls.

"Well, if we don't find the study soon, this might
do." Lytton sounded hopeful.

Moreland thought his friend might be tired. He
was, after all, recently an invalid. He tried the next
room with some impatience, and was relieved to
find it the one he'd been seeking. "Here we are at
last." He stood aside and permitted Lytton to
precede him into the study.

"Would you care for brandy?"

"Yes, by George. Though I don't mind having
missed it after dinner for Lady Valerie's sake, I
think it would hit the spot just about now."

Moreland found the bellpull and gave it a firm
yank. He shot a wry glance at Lytton. "We'll see if
that does any good."

They moved to the desk, Moreland to the working side, and Lytton to the chair facing him. Both
looked around the study. It was a cozy room, half
the size of Moreland's study at his London house,
which was the smallest of all his studies. There
were only a few bookcases, but their absence was
readily explained by the double doors in one wall.
Since they had already blundered into the room on
the other side of those doors, Moreland knew it was
the library—a handy arrangement.

There was a brisk knock on the door. It opened, and the young butler stood there. "You rang, milord?"

"Brandy, please, Wilson."

"Certainly, Your Lordship." The boy—Moreland couldn't help thinking of him as such—bowed and left.

"Deuced young for a butler, wouldn't you say, Moreland?"

The Viscount frowned. "I'd thought the same thing." He shrugged with a smile. "Well, after the life we have led, I suppose it will make little difference, so long as he can find the brandy."

Perseus made all haste to the kitchen, where he found the entire family helping Cook with the kitchen chores. One look at his flushed face, and they were instantly on the alert.

"Get the decanter. I'll find some brandy." With that he put his shoulder to a set of shelves in the corner of the huge room and moved it aside to reveal the doorway to a hidden cellar. A breath of sea air issued from it.

Andromeda hurried out to find the decanter, while Rosalind ran over to the doorway through which Perseus had disappeared. "Perseus! Wouldn't you like a light?"

"No, thank you, Roz. I know where everything is down here." There was the sound of flesh connecting with something solid and a muffled, "Damn!"

"Are you all right?" Rosalind gestured for Cassie to bring the lamp from the center of the kitchen table.

"Fine," Perseus snarled, reappearing before

Cassie could comply. There was a small keg in one of his hands. The other rubbed his bruised shin, making his progress hobbled and awkward.

Rosalind and Andy, who'd rushed back in with a cut-crystal decanter, exchanged a glance, then contented themselves with polishing the decanter and a pair of glasses as well as any barkeep might have done. Any amusement they might have felt, they kept carefully in check. Luckily, the shadows cast by the ruffles on their mobcaps hid the laughter in their eyes.

Tom Coachman spoke from where he was enjoying his pipe in the chimney corner. "Take a lantern next time, laddie."

His wife chimed in, "Aye, Your Lordship. You could break your neck in those passages that lead down to the sea. You must be more careful. You're the head of the family now, and all rely on you." Cook spoke with quiet authority, pausing respectfully from her work to do so.

Perseus stood still as a statue as her comment registered. He was silent a moment, then said with dignity, "Thank you, Mrs. Freep." The moment passed and he grinned at her. "The family is so unaware of my consequence that I had quite forgotten it, myself."

"Well," snapped Andromeda, "the time to wallow in it is not yet upon you, My Lord Butler!" She shoved the decanter and two glasses toward him on a silver tray. "You had best hurry. It is a long way back up to the study."

After quickly filling the decanter, Perseus seized the tray and left the kitchen. Evidently it was not only a prophet who was without honor in his own home!

Their glasses filled and the quill sharpened to suit Moreland, the two men regarded each other across the desk. "Where best to begin?" Moreland queried.

Lytton took a sip of his brandy. "Hmmm," he said appreciatively. "Lord Winston must have a fine cellar if this is any indication."

Moreland nodded absently, his mind on the matter at hand. "We must get to know the local gentry. How?" He looked morosely at Lytton.

Lytton frowned in concentration. "Shall we—and by that I mean you—have them all for dinner?"

"Good, but even if we had them twenty at a time, too slow. Dinner isn't long enough, and one only gets to talk to those on either side."

"Card party? What about a ball?"

"Same problem. Limited time to get to know the guests." Moreland ran a hand through his night-dark hair.

Lytton frowned, thinking hard. "An al fresco affair, then. With games of some sort. That could take all day and we could move about and talk with everyone present."

"Yes, that would do." He made a note. "I suppose we could have a ball to introduce Valerie to the neighbors, but I hate to honor the chit just now. She is in disgrace, after all."

"Ah, but she is not to appear to be, is that not so?"

"You have a point."

"One that we might use to advantage later, I think." Lytton smiled.

"Indeed." Moreland grinned back. "A series of parties for my sister might be just the thing to insinuate us into the neighborhood. An excellent plan, Lytton. Good man!"

Moreland saw that Lytton frowned and knew instinctively that his friend wondered if he had deliberately waited for him to suggest a plan. He suppressed a sigh. It was going to be difficult to make Lytton realize that he was still useful—the man was so dead set against admitting it.

Moreland fervently hoped he would be able to accomplish the self-imposed task.

Chapter 8

"Only a moment more, please." Moreland made his request without looking up from the paper he was rapidly covering with his distinctive handwriting.

Rosalind stood quietly in front of the desk in the study, awaiting the Viscount's instructions. She liked the deep timbre of his voice and his obvious good manners.

As she waited for him to finish the last few lines of his letter, she permitted her eyes to travel his person.

His broad shoulders were clad in a blue superfine coat easily recognized as being Weston's creation. With it he wore a plain, deep yellow vest, and his pristine white cravat was arranged in a style that might be the envy of every man in the *ton*. These she skimmed over lightly.

It was the man himself who held her interest. She liked his broad forehead and determined chin. His nose was straight and rather attractive, but it was his mouth, with its finely chiseled lips, that held her attention.

She was certain his eyes would be his best feature, but just now they were cast down in consideration of his written words, and she was unable to see them. She'd been so nervous when they'd met previously that she had not remarked them.

She smiled to herself. What marvelous freedom there was in being a servant! Never before had she been granted the opportunity to study someone of the opposite gender so minutely. Had he known she was the Countess Winston, Moreland would have been forced to pay her every attention. She, in turn, would have had to be very sure not to stare as she was doing now.

She found she enjoyed staring. At least, she enjoyed staring at Lord Moreland.

Suddenly, as if feeling her regard, Moreland looked up. She kept her expression calm and inquiring as his gaze locked with hers. After a moment, he reached for the chased silver receptacle filled with fine sand and shook it over his letter, still regarding her. His eyes were clear, bright blue, and full of intelligence. Clearly they *were* his best feature.

"Mrs. Rose." He shook the sand from his letter, then slipped the paper into the top drawer of the desk.

"Your Lordship?"

"I have decided to have a party for the neighboring gentry." As he spoke his long-fingered hands restored the writing things to their proper places. His gaze, however, never left her face. "I do not know my neighbors and must ask you to be so kind as to give me the names of all those who live within a day's drive of the castle. I shall invite those closest the sea first, so I would appreciate your putting them at the top of your list."

Rosalind knew she must respond, but his request threw her thoughts into a tangle. The neighbors. How she missed so many of them—the Shaws, Lord and Lady Chadwick, the Vicar and his cheerful young wife. She was deluged with waves of nostalgia.

She felt her face first blanch and immediately blush. How flustered she was even to think of them and of her youth here on the seaswept coast. They must not see her! Many of them had known her well before her marriage and would be sure to recognize her. Nor must they see the rest of the "staff" at Castle Winston! Suppose someone recognized one of the "servants" who were Winstons in disguise? *Good heavens,* she thought, her head spinning. *What am I to do?* She felt the blood drain from her face. *My father would be devastated!*

"Mrs. Rose." The Viscount got up and came around the desk to her. "Are you ill?"

"No. No. Not at all. I . . . I was just going over in my mind the number of people I can recall." Her voice lost its uncertainty, steadied, and regained strength. "I am sure that I shall be able to come up with the list you require with Miss Evans's help."

"You are certain you are all right? Would you like some brandy?" He made a move in the direction of the drink table against the wall.

Rosalind detained him with a hand on his arm. "You are most kind," she said, her voice strangely husky. She had not been treated to such courtesy even once in her position at the Ledbetter house, and she was oddly touched by his concern. She smiled up at him, momentarily forgetting her role of servant, unaware that she was treating him as an equal.

Moreland was not unaware, however. Her dazzling smile and the light touch of her hand on his sleeve shook him. He sought desperately for a comment and could only come up with "Who is Miss Evans?"

His brows drew down in a puzzled frown that had little to do with his question. She was so beautiful, this woman who stood so easily beside him. And she was confident. Confident with a confidence that went beyond that of a servant. Was she a gentlewoman reduced to servitude by some vagary of fate, or was she something else? Was she at ease with him because she had been too much at ease with some other gentleman of high rank?

He stared down at her. Her wide gray eyes were like pools in the mist, their long lashes tipped with gold. Her skin was perfection. Even as near as he had come to her in his concern for her welfare—so near he could smell the fresh flower scent of her—he could detect not the slightest flaw. Her lips were rosy and soft, inviting a man to . . .

He yanked himself back in line viciously, mentally cursing himself for a cad. Shamed by his foul thought that she might have been someone's mistress as well as by his own quickened pulse, he hardly realized she was answering his question.

"Oh, dear. Of course you have not met Miss Evans yet, have you?"

Moreland saw she was sufficiently overset by his inquiry that she had not noticed his reaction to her proximity. *Thank God for small favors!* He used her momentary confusion to reseat himself at his desk. "No," he forced himself to say dryly, "I have not had that pleasure."

"Well—" Rosalind took a deep breath and set about explaining Miss Evans's plausibility. "Miss Evans is the retired housekeeper of the castle." She put her hands behind her so the Viscount could not see her crossed fingers. Lying did not come easily to her, but she forged ahead, embellishing. "Miss Evans is here to help train the staff. Myself included."

Moreland interrupted her, one eyebrow raised, making his expression cynical. "It would seem that this interview is going to take longer than I had thought. Won't you be seated, Mrs. Rose."

It wasn't a question as to her preference, and she knew it. It was an order to seat herself and prepare for an inquisition. She took the chair opposite him with a rustle of her gray taffeta skirt, still hiding her crossed fingers.

"Mrs. Rose." He let his voice sound censorious. "I find myself somewhat at a loss to hear that my housekeeper—temporarily mine, of course—is in need of training." He looked to her for the next remark, his blue eyes somber.

She drew herself up and looked him straight in the eye. "It is merely a matter of making me familiar with the way things are done here at the castle, Your Lordship. I can assure you that I am well able to manage the running of the house." *Well, that much is true anyway. When but a girl I oversaw the running of the one next door.* That thought heartened her.

Moreland started to speak, evidently thought better of it, and regarded her silently for a long moment. Rosalind met his eyes unflinchingly. The only sign that he might be causing her some distress was her heightened color.

He decided to save his questions about the castle staff for later. "Please have that list for me as soon as possible, Mrs. Rose."

"Certainly, Your Lordship." She spoke with quiet dignity.

"Thank you, Mrs. Rose," he said, releasing her from his presence, and wondered if he was imagining that it was all she could do not to leap from her chair and run from the room.

He knew he was not imagining the relief with which she said, "Thank *you*, Your Lordship."

Long after she had gone, the Eighth Viscount Moreland sat staring at the door she had closed behind her. Would he really have kissed his housekeeper?

Chapter 9

Night was falling, and Perseus and one of the footmen were making the rounds of the house, lighting the candles in the various rooms the Forsythes and Lieutenant Lytton had formed the habit of frequenting. They had just turned into the hall leading to the library and study when Perseus stopped and cocked his head to listen.

The faint sound of a horse coming fast up the long gravel drive sent him to the door. "Alert Frank to see to this horse, Jim. Sounds as if he'll need a long walk to cool him out." He threw open the door to the noise of iron-shod hooves slithering across the flagstones at the bottom of the steps.

A man vaulted from the saddle, ran up the stairs, and demanded, "Take me to Viscount Moreland immediately."

Under his imperturbable pose as butler, Perseus burned at the man's ill treatment of his mount. Without deigning to reply, he turned and led the way to a small anteroom. "Wait here." He'd have said, "please wait here," if the man had not been so careless of the comfort of his worn-out horse.

He left the man fuming and went to inform Moreland of his presence. He met the Viscount descending the stairs. "Your Lordship, there is a person who wishes to see you. I have put him in the green anteroom."

"A person, eh?" Moreland grinned at his butler. "By that I take it you do not care for his appearance?"

Perseus permitted himself an answering smile. "I didn't care for his neglect of his horse," he admitted.

"But you have had it seen to?"

"Of course, Your Lordship!" Perseus was startled that Moreland would ask.

Moreland looked at the youth speculatively. The boy's smile had given him the look of an eager sixteen-year-old. "Please find Lieutenant Lytton and send him to me in the study."

"Certainly, Your Lordship." Perseus bowed and took the stairs two at a time in search of the Lieutenant.

Moreland paused with his hand on the handle of the door to the green anteroom. He shook his head. Did the butler have to bound up the stairs like that? Wasn't it bad enough that the boy hardly had to shave?

In the study after the messenger from Attleborough had been sent to bed in the servant's quarters, Moreland watched Lytton reading the dispatch. Both men were tight-lipped.

"So he's done it again." Lytton looked up into his friend's bleak eyes.

"Yes, and no one would have known the documents had been removed from where they belonged if Attleborough hadn't put that pinch of cobweb with them."

"At your suggestion, I recall."

Moreland shrugged off the credit. "We can try, but I have little hope of apprehending the spy before he can escape the country. There are miles of coast, and we have no idea who he might be." He slammed his hand down on the desk in frustration. "Blast it, we're moving too slowly." He took a quick, long-strided turn around the study. "We must begin the business of looking over our neighbors. I'll send out invitations tomorrow." He looked at Lytton. "What the devil can we do on short notice?"

Lytton grinned at him. "Women always decide these things. That's a question for Valerie, isn't it?"

Moreland quirked an eyebrow at him. "You can't be serious."

Lytton shrugged, smiling.

Just then Valerie breezed into the room. "What is it Lytton can't be serious about?"

Her brother said smoothly, "About asking you what sort of entertainment we could put on for the neighbors on short notice."

"Lytton!" Valerie stared at him hard, her expression just short of a scowl. "I *attend* parties. I do *not* plan them. Besides, I came in merely to bid you good night." She smiled at them. "You will be sure to put me at the top of the list of those invited, though, won't you?" With a saucy flirt of her shoulder, she left them to their dilemma.

Moreland raised an inquiring eyebrow at Lytton.

Lytton said, "Hmmmm, yes. I see. Perhaps Mrs. Rose?"

"It's worth an attempt." Moreland crossed the room and pulled the tapestry bellpull. When Perseus, whom the Viscount knew as Wilson—a name chosen because it was close to the young Lord's own and thus might avoid confusion—appeared, Moreland sent him to fetch the housekeeper.

"Kindly ask Mrs. Rose if she would do us the favor of attending us here, Wilson."

"Of course, Your Lordship."

As he went to do as he was bid, he wondered what the deuce Moreland could want with Rosalind. He wondered, too, what Rosalind would say to being asked to the study at so late an hour.

He found her turning down the bed in the Viscount's room. "I say, Roz. Isn't Andy supposed to be the chambermaid?"

"Yes, Pers. And she does a splendid job keeping the rooms clean and the linens fresh."

"Well then. Where is she now?"

Rosalind colored slightly. "I prefer to turn the beds down myself."

"You do enough already, what with the time you spend supervising everything and the time you spend helping Cook prepare the meals." He held the door open for her when she was ready to leave the room, then trailed after to Lytton's bedchamber. "Let Andy do this."

"No," Rosalind said softly, turning to face him

squarely. "She is so young and lovely. It is better that I do this."

Perseus frowned as he realized what she was getting at, and what she must have seen or experienced during the years she was without the protection of family. Even as his heart ached for her, he had to tell her, "I say, Roz. Moreland and Lytton are honorable men."

"I certainly hope so. In fact I believe they are. But there is always the chance that one might have too much wine." She let the subject drop. "Did you want me?"

"Drat! Yes. Moreland wants you in the study."

"At this hour? How odd." She hurried to the stairwell and rushed down the steps, leaving Perseus to return to his own duties.

"You wished to see me, Your Lordship?"

With some difficulty Moreland gave up his perusal of the color in her cheeks, and the way her lips were slightly parted to facilitate her breathing after her rush to answer his summons. What was it about this woman? What was it that lurked at the corner of his mind and slid away when he tried to recall it? Ignoring the rise and fall of her bosom, he answered, "Yes, Mrs. Rose. Lieutenant Lytton and I are very much in need of your assistance."

"I hope I shall be able to help."

"We feel certain that you will, Mrs. Rose," Lytton said with his charming smile.

"We require a suggestion." Moreland smiled at her. "We wish to put on some sort of entertainment that we can do almost immediately, entertaining a maximum number of guests."

Rosalind cast back in her mind for some memory of the entertainments her father had provided for his guests. She strove to discover one that would not overtax the abilities of the skeleton staff at Castle Winston. Finally something came to mind that might do. "If Your Lordship would not mind a very country entertainment, we could have a lawn party with a pig roast. They are very popular during fairs and harvest homes, and would be a simple thing to do with a small staff."

Moreland looked to Lytton. Both thought it would do. "An excellent idea, Mrs. Rose. Easy on the kitchen, for they have only the side dishes that can't be done over the open fire. I imagine there is some man who is skilled at such things that we might hire?"

"I believe Mr. Talley still does pig roasts, Your Lordship. The last I heard he was the best. And he brings his two sons to help him."

"Good! A lawn party with a pig roast it shall be."

Lytton said dryly, "Val will have a fit."

Moreland looked grim. "Too bad."

"Some of your new neighbors may think it a rather informal entry into their midst," Lytton remarked.

Rosalind interrupted, "I think not, sirs. This is the country, after all, and you can always say you chose this sort of party in order to quickly make their acquaintance."

"Have you made me the list I requested?"

"It is almost complete, Your Lordship." Rosalind hoped she had everyone on it. She wanted another chance to check it with the castle regulars, however.

"When you have it complete, I wish you will

send invitations to all on it. Get my sister to help you write them. She has a passable hand."

With subtle emphasis Rosalind replied, "I shall be pleased *to assist* Lady Valerie in writing the invitations, Your Lordship."

A faint line of annoyance creased his forehead. He let her reprimand go for something more important. "May I ask you to be seated and to write a sentence for me."

"Certainly, Your Lordship," she said stiffly. She moved around the desk, took his chair, and reached for the quill. Though she was, of course, proficient with a goose quill, she much preferred a pen, and made a mental note to use the gold-nibbed one she had upstairs among her things when the time came to address the invitations.

She wrote quickly, replaced the quill in its stand, then handed the paper to the Viscount as she rose to take her former place on the other side of the desk.

He glanced at it and said in a bemused voice, "Thank you. This will do nicely."

"Will that be all, Your Lordship?"

"Thank you, yes." His eyes never left the sample he had required of her handwriting. He heard the rustle of her skirt as it whispered across the study to the door. He heard her softly close the door behind her before he could tear his attention from the paper in his hand.

Passing it to his friend he asked, "Now, what the devil do you make of that, Lytton?"

Chapter 10

Lytton looked long at the paper Moreland had handed him. "A lovely example of a lady's handwriting. As for the words, I don't know what to make of 'em." He passed the paper back to his friend. "Never was too bright about those things at school, you know. Head too full of the glory to be won in the army." His voice fell silent on a bitter note, as his glance brushed the empty sleeve that was tucked neatly into his belt at his left side.

"The words say, 'Wisdom sometimes is found in folly,'" Moreland told him.

"Some new writer?"

"Hardly. Fifteen B.C. From the *Odes*." He stared at the neat elegance of her handwriting, bemused. What the devil did she mean by writing that?

"So it *was* Greek. I was a rotten Greek scholar, but the *Odes* were by Horace, were they not?"

"Yes." His voice told Lytton that his mind was far away.

"I say, Edward. Where have you gone wandering?"

"Sorry. I quite agree. She writes very nicely. I'm sure she will do a competent job on the invitations."

"Competent? Well, let me tell you, she is bound to do better than Valerie. You should try reading *her* handwriting by the light of a campfire. Enough to make a man go blind, her scrawl is."

"Oh, did Valerie write you while you were away?"

"Yes, bless the little scamp." He smiled like an indulgent uncle. "I read some of her letters over and over. She brightened some gloomy times with her chatter. Writes just like she talks."

"Not like she talks now, I hope." Moreland shuddered to think what Valerie's constant petulance would do to an embattled soldier's morale.

"She does seem a bit—" Lytton broke off with a frown, unable to find the word he wanted.

"Sour, complaining, demanding, and discontent?" the lady's older brother inquired politely.

"Oh, come now, Edward! She is just high-spirited. And the isolation of this castle from all she enjoys in London must weigh heavily on her." Lytton's handsome face was married by a frown. "She is a beautiful little thing, you know."

"Beauty is not an excuse for unpleasantness. Or irresponsibility." Moreland's voice was implacable.

Lytton started to speak and thought better of it. He took a deep breath and another subject. "Doesn't it seem strange that a mere housekeeper can write in Greek?"

"I have the distinct feeling that our Mrs. Rose is

anything *but* a mere anything," Moreland answered with a faraway look in his eye.

"Perseus! I have just done the most asinine thing."

"I sincerely doubt that you could do anything even approaching the asinine, Roz. What have you done?" Perseus poured her a cup of tea from the pot he had just had Cook brew. "Here, come sit a minute." He held a chair for her at the head of the long trestle table.

Rosalind sank into it gracefully. "Moreland asked for a sample of my handwriting to see whether I could be trusted not to disgrace him in the addressing of invitations." She shot him an apologetic look. "For some reason, it irritated me to give it."

"So?"

"So I wrote 'Wisdom is sometimes found in folly.' " She looked at him ruefully. "I suppose I was thinking of our masquerade and how clever it was of Andy to think of it as a way to save all the money from the lease to do repairs and such."

"And?"

"Well, besides the fact that some gentlemen might think I was inviting them to fall prey to a little folly, I wrote it in Greek."

Perseus slopped the pouring of his own cup of tea. "Surely you did not!"

Rosalind merely nodded miserably.

Perseus frowned a moment, then instructed, "Merely tell him it was a phrase you learned by rote. One that showed off your penmanship to advantage. Tell him you haven't any idea what it means."

"A little silly, but I suppose it will suffice . . . if he should show any interest." She smiled tentatively at Perseus. "I suppose I'm just . . ."

He finished for her, "And just don't know what, eh?"

She laughed.

"Look, Roz. You're worn out with keeping all of us from making a fatal mistake. Why don't you take a ride tomorrow? That'll get the cobwebs out. Just go early enough to miss any of our guests."

"Would it be all right, do you think?"

"Of course. Take Andy's mare. Cassie's is in foal to Hermes's charger."

"No! Really? I'd almost forgotten I'd sent him home to you. I never knew he got here. Thunderer, and Sergeant MacFie with him."

Perseus saw the light in her face and smiled. "MacFie's still with us, he just never comes up from the stables."

"Oh, how I should like to see him again!"

"Are you sure it won't make you sad, Roz? The fear that he might stir up hurtful memories is what keeps him away."

"What utter nonsense! I would dearly love to see his funny old face once again." The day's weariness forgotten, she sprang up from the table. "Come take me to him!"

"Whoa! It's late, *ma chère belle soeur*. Let the man sleep. You'll see him in the morning."

None of the joy left her face. "Of course. What a thoughtless beast I am." She stood beaming at him. "Oh, Perseus, how splendid it will be to see him again."

"You look like a schoolgirl expecting a treat." He

rose, smiling. "I think now it's time for bed. If you're going to sneak in a ride, tomorrow will be an extra long day for you. You'll need a full night's sleep." Slipping an arm about her, he steered her toward the steps up out of the kitchen.

"Yes, Your Lordship." She smiled up at him. "I hear and obey."

In the study, Moreland sat alone. He, too, had been thoughtful of his friend's weariness and sent Lytton off to bed.

The piece of heavy vellum stationery lay on the desk in front of him. The fine hand of his housekeeper held a great fascination for him. Who had taught her to write so beautifully? And in Greek! Why? Wouldn't it be enough for a servant—albeit an upper servant—to be able to make lists and write replies to her employer's directives? Why would a mere housekeeper have to have the handwriting of a duchess?

And why in heaven's name did it matter to *him*?

Sighing audibly, Moreland stood and snuffed the candles in the candelabra on his desk one by careful one. Then he did the candles on the mantel. The room in darkness except for the light from the dying fire, he walked to the door.

Abruptly he turned again, seeming to have made up his mind about something. Walking rapidly back to the desk, he snatched up the paper from its tooled-leather top and, folding it, shoved it into his coat.

Shaking his head over his own folly, he exited the room at last, and strode rapidly down the hall to the grand staircase. As he ascended the stairs, he called himself every kind of a fool for going back for the paper.

He made no move, however, to rid himself of it. When he arrived at his bedchamber, he gave one seemingly cursory glance around. Discovering he was alone, he took the piece of stationery from inside his coat and quickly slipped it under his pillow.

An instant later, the tall figure of his valet filled the dressing room door as he emerged to help Moreland prepare for bed.

Chapter 11

"Well, there is something to be said for the hours I keep as a servant. It has become an easy thing to rise well before my 'betters,' and I shall get my ride in!" Rosalind considered her reflection in her looking glass and mentally thanked whichever distant Winston had made such comfortable quarters for his housekeeper.

The mirrored surface showed her a trim young lady of quality in a slightly outmoded riding habit of a deep gray that nicely set off her eyes. Adding to their sparkle, a white ostrich plume on the habit's matching military shako curled down one side of her face and under her chin. She toyed with the idea of removing it as it was certainly too fine, even for an upper servant.

"No one will be up to see you, goose!" She smiled at the serious face that looked back at her. "Besides, with *your* sewing ability, you would probably destroy the whole hat trying to remove the feather."

She caught up her gloves and crop. The gloves were supple light-gray kidskin, not the York tan that was *de rigueur* for fashion. Rosalind had always preferred to set her own fashion.

Letting herself out into the barely candlelit hall, she sped down the stairs and out to the stables.

Perseus must have arranged for her ride, for her mount was waiting in the predawn gloom when she reached the stables. She was sharply reminded how much she missed visiting stables with their wonderful smells of well-cared-for leather and smooth-coated horses. Breathing in the sweet scent of hay, she felt such a lift of her spirits that she was sure the groom holding the mare must think she'd taken leave of her senses.

Putting her foot into his waiting hand, she was tossed up and landed lightly in the saddle. As she hooked her right leg over the leaping horn, she gathered her reins and thanked the boy for guiding the stirrup onto her left boot. She arranged her skirt carefully, then nodded to signal her readiness to ride.

Smiling shyly, the groom pulled his forelock and stepped back, letting go of her bridle.

The mare was fresh and playing up, but Rosalind handled her easily, keeping her to a walk—albeit a dancing one—until she had warmed up a little. Reaching the end of the long drive, she let the impatient mare have her head. Instantly the fine animal set off running and bucking playfully.

Rosalind grabbed her hat just before it would have left her head and cried, "Oh, no! You've overrated my abilities, pretty miss!" Rosalind pulled her in and settled her down to an easy canter. The mare tried to argue, pulling lightly at the bit in a series of quick snatches. Rosalind, long deprived of a chance for a ride, had no desire to end this one so soon by measuring her length on the cliff top and refused to oblige the mare by letting her have more rein.

The mare—how Rosalind wished she had asked her name—settled nicely. Cantering along beside the sea that crashed against the headland many feet below, Rosalind felt as if her heart would leap from her body for sheer joy. The wind was behind her, but the speed of the mare's passage made it seem as if she rode into it, and the smoothness of the animal's gait made her feel she had wings.

Finally breathless, she asked the mare to walk. Obedient to her fine training, the animal slowed through a few steps of a jogging trot to a comfortable, long-strided walk.

"Oh, you beauty! How kind they are to let me ride you!" She breathed deeply of the crisp sea air, the salt tang of it bringing back poignant memories of her childhood here on these very cliffs. She watched the gulls wheeling and turning, only a few yards away, their strong white wings still on the air as they rode the currents near the cliffs.

The mare pretended never to have seen gulls before. With a snort and a plunging jump away from the cliff edge, she protested their presence.

Rosalind soothed her with a few low words and a steady hand, reveling in the lithe movement under her. "If you were mine, pretty girl, I would have to see for myself whether a person had good hands before I would lend you." She patted the mare on her neck, noticing the veins that stood out on it. Quickly she stripped off a glove, and leaning precariously, felt to see if the horse were over-heated. Pleased that she was not, she pulled her glove back on. "Oh, what a splendid girl you are!"

The sun was coming up, shining across the Channel, glinting off the waves and dazzling her eyes till she could barely make out the gulls mewing in the pale rosy sky. The pearly light by which they had come was quickly giving way to the brighter light of a new day.

Dawn meant the housemaids would be up about the business of cleaning the castle, and that meant that she must be there in her place as supervisor, as well. With a sigh, she turned her mount back toward Castle Winston.

As the mare turned, Rosalind caught a movement out of the corner of her eye. A solitary figure, that of a man, walked the cliff top to the north of her. She halted her horse and watched him over her shoulder. Her heart became heavy with longing as he came striding purposefully forward, his head bent against the wind.

Having recognized her father, Rosalind was suddenly filled with emotions with which she was unwilling to cope. Relieved he was not close enough to identify her, she touched her heel to the mare and let her bound away toward home. The pleasure of her ride was gone, stolen by sad memories of the past.

Walking the last mile home to cool the mare, she had time to indulge in a few tears and wipe them resolutely away. If she had been given a fresh chance to do it all again, there was nothing she would do differently. "There is no use in crying over spilt milk, Rosalind!" she reminded herself sternly.

She straightened in her saddle and put her mind firmly to enjoying the last few minutes left before she reached the stables. The mare caught her determined mood and moved more confidently beneath her.

At the stables, an old friend awaited her. "Milady!" MacFie beamed broadly. "Good to see you again." With the easy familiarity of an old friend, he reached up his hands to span her trim waist and lifted her from the saddle as if she were a feather.

"MacFie!" She gave him a great hug. "Oh, what a happy thing it is to see your face again!" She blinked back tears and said, "You look wonderful!" Cocking her head, she asked, "Has life been treating you well, MacFie?"

"Indeed it has, milady. A fine, snug place you sent me to when you bid me bring home himself's charger."

"You decided to stay, then. I am so glad."

"Where else would I be going, Milady? With himself gone?"

She turned then, quickly, so he wouldn't see her tears, and started for the house, calling back to him, "I'm Mrs. Rose, the housekeeper, MacFie. Remember it, please." She waved jauntily and walked swiftly away.

A man, tall and broad, came out of the shadows of the barn and joined MacFie. "There goes a brave lady," he said. "And even more beautiful than the last time I saw her."

MacFie turned and fastened interested eyes on the newcomer. "And just when," he demanded of his new friend, "might that have been?"

Chapter 12

Moreland woke feeling well rested and more than ready to tackle the planning of his party. He rushed Gates through the morning ritual of dressing him until the big valet was ready to tear his hair. And he wasn't completely sure it was his own he wanted to tear!

Finally released from the care of his valet, Moreland went in search of his housekeeper. He almost literally ran into Wilson as the butler came out of the drawing room. "Have you seen Mrs. Rose, Wilson?"

"Not since breakfast, Your Lordship."

"If you should see her, would you kindly tell her I am waiting for her in the study."

"Certainly, Your Lordship. Would you like me to go find her for you?" Perseus was determined to be a perfect butler, aware that the Viscount looked at him askance because of his youth.

"That won't be necessary. I'm sure you'll bump

into her before long, thank you, Wilson." The Viscount strode down the hall toward the study.

Perseus stood gazing after him and wondering why the Viscount seemed so confused. First he wanted his housekeeper, then it was of no importance. That was very odd behavior in a man like Moreland. He shook his head. The thing that was beginning to worry him was that His Lordship always seemed to be in need of Rosalind of late.

Rosalind was counting out sheets when Perseus found her. After lifting the last set of fresh ones into Cassie's waiting arms, she closed the tall door of the linen closet and relocked it. A whisper of lavender and rosemary lingered for a moment in the wide hall.

"I say, Roz."

She turned, smiling. "Yes, dear?" She laughed and corrected herself. "No, I must say '*Yes, Mr. Wilson?*'"

"Whatever you say, *I'd* like to say that I'd jolly well like to know why Moreland wants you in the study again. Seems every time I turn around he's asking for you."

Rosalind smiled at him afresh. "It's his entertainment."

"What!" Perseus was outraged.

"No!" Rosalind laughed merrily. "I don't mean he amuses himself by running me around at his beck and call, you widgeon." She patted his cheek. "I mean the entertainment he plans to give, of course. He will want to know if I have readied the list for the invitations." She frowned slightly, looking at him earnestly. "I have been away so long that

I may not have all the neighbors on it. Will you come along to my room and glance at the list before I take it to him?"

Perseus obligingly trailed her to her quarters. After a swift perusal he said, "There are a few new people in the neighborhood since you and Hermes left. A Mr. Radley, another Mister named Cox who has quite a large brood of daughters and a hatchet-faced wife. Probably in inverse order, however." He rolled his eyes. "The daughters make me happy I'm a *penniless* peer," he threw in as an aside. "Then there is Lord Alton. Radley and Alton are single gentlemen, I believe."

"Very well, I shall add them to the list." Rosalind sat down at the tiny desk by the window and, using her pen, added the three names to the bottom of her list. "Oh, dear." She remembered that the Viscount wanted the seaside names on top. "Do any of them live on the shore?"

"Alton does—he bought the Murreys' summer place."

Rosalind recalled the small property, that her own grandfather had deeded to one of his solicitors, who had become his great friend. Old Murrey's daughter must be gone, then. She was sorry. She fondly remembered hot scones and wonderful strong tea, and a woman with no children of her own who had been happy to take time with a lonely little Lady. She snatched herself back to what Pers was telling her.

"So does Mr. Radley, I believe. Bought the Clarges' manor house down coast and refurbished it. Seems to be rolling in the ready." Perseus's envy of Mr. Radley's financial status showed in his voice.

"Drat! Then I shall have to scratch them through and squeeze them in at the top. It's going to make my list look quite sloppy."

"Good."

"Good? How can you say so?" She looked up, startled, at Perseus.

"Perhaps it'll make up for your pedantic flight of fancy."

"My ped . . . Oh, of course, the Greek." She stared in consternation at the list. "Let's hope you are right!"

In the study, Rosalind presented the list to Moreland the moment he acknowledged her presence.

He cocked an inquiring eyebrow as he accepted it.

"It is the list you asked of me. I hope it is complete. At any rate, I have done my best and have had it checked over by Per . . . Mr. Wilson."

"Thank you, Mrs. Rose." Moreland studied it briefly, then said, "You write an exceedingly fine hand." He looked at her searchingly for a long moment. Finally he added, "My sister does not write as well."

Rosalind thought it wiser not to comment on this. It is one thing for a person to criticize their own, but quite another for a servant to agree. Or anyone else for that matter. Even if that one *has* spent a great deal of time trying to decipher the writing on notes of instruction sent her by Lady Valerie from time to time.

Moreland stared at her speculatively. Finally he asked, "Tell me, Mrs. Rose, how is it a housekeeper writes Greek?" He regarded her steadily from piercing blue eyes.

The lie Perseus had concocted about attractive convolutions rose easily to her lips and stuck there. She looked him full in the face and told him the truth, even while a part of her mind quailed at it. "I am the only child of my father. He is an educated man, and in the absence of sons had me educated as if I were one."

"Latin, too."

She nodded solemnly, "My father believes that, 'education makes greater difference between man and man than nature has made between man and brute.'"

He heard the quotation marks in her statement and raised an eyebrow.

"John Adams, an American farmer, wrote that to his wife. My father heard it while in Boston."

"It would seem your father sympathized with the rebels."

"My father sympathizes with men of learning. As a soldier he could not possibly sympathize with rebels."

"Many good Englishmen did."

"They didn't have to order them shot at."

He quirked an eyebrow. "Your father was an officer, then."

Rosalind was giving away much more than she wished to. "Yes."

Moreland understood by the monosyllable that she had no wish to elaborate. He had already far overstepped the bounds of polite conversation between master and servant, he would question her no more.

"Please send out invitations for the lawn party today. Choose the earliest date possible." He returned to his correspondence with a brusque, "Thank you."

Rosalind said a low "Yes, Your Lordship," and left the study, slightly confused. It would seem Moreland thought she was to usurp Lady Valerie's place. That would hardly be proper!

She made her decision in a flash and went in search of the young lady. Finding her reading in the chair next to the window in the morning room, she waited until she was noticed.

"Did you want to see me, Mrs. Rose?"

Rosalind selected her words carefully. "Your brother would like the invitations sent for his lawn party. He thought I might help you in writing them." She smiled at the pretty blonde, wishing she could offer the lovely girl companionship. "I shall be glad to help if you should like me to." There. That would do nicely.

"Oh, very well." Valerie put her book down on the windowsill. "If we must, we must. Do you think the dining room table would be a good place?"

"As good as any." Rosalind gave the girl an encouraging smile. "I shall get the writing things and join you there."

"Oh, no, I'll come along and help you."

Rosalind was startled. For the first time she really looked at the girl. Her lovely blue eyes had a sadness about them that Rosalind had never noticed before. Could it be that she was lonely? Well, why not? She was miles from home, as well as the only female around the place except for servants. Suddenly her heart went out to the girl.

"There is a large desk in the library we might use, if you would prefer," she offered. "No one uses it for anything just now, and we could write and leave things there without having them disturbed should we not finish them all at one sitting."

Valerie smiled at her. It wasn't the mechanical, unseeing smile of a mistress to a servant, but a real—and suddenly warm—smile. "Yes, I think that might be better."

Rosalind carefully gave way so that Valerie walked first down the hall to the library. When they reached the room, Rosalind stepped forward and opened the door for her. Inside, she pulled the bellpull. "Shall I have a footman freshen the fire?" she asked as she moved around the room opening drapes to admit more light. "We keep these closed when no one is using the library so that the sunlight does not fade the bindings on the book spines." Oh, dear. Now that she was thinking of Valerie as a lonely girl, she found herself behaving in much the same way Miss Murrey had to her when she was a lonely, unhappy child. Miss Murrey had always explained at length because she felt it helped equip one for life to learn all that one could.

But Lady Valerie wasn't a child to be taught, and she wasn't thought to be an unhappy child. Her reputation of late was that of an overspoiled, pampered darling of society who refused to behave always with propriety. Seeing the droop of the girl's mouth, Rosalind began to wonder about her. Was she really petulant, or was the child genuinely unhappy? Rosalind realized that she was making up her own mind about Valerie, regardless of society's assessment.

Valerie sat in the chair behind the desk, and Rosalind told Frank, who answered her summons, to pull up a chair for her. "Then freshen the fire, please. It is still chilly in here from the night."

"Yes, ma'am. The castle walls hold the cold a long while. Come summer, you'll find it a blessing, but for now, a fire's the thing."

Valerie looked at the footman's broad back in astonishment. She wasn't used to such talkative servants.

"Will that be all, Mrs. Rose?"

"Yes, thank you, Frank." She made a mental note to teach the footmen that even if it were she who sent for and gave them orders, it was to the ranking person present they must speak. Fortunately, Lady Valerie took no offense. She was already thinking of the invitations.

"What shall we say?" Valerie looked to her for the answer.

Rosalind smiled, pulled a piece of stationery to her, and wrote a quick, rough draft of what she thought Moreland wanted to convey in his invitation. She had just passed it to Valerie when Lieutenant Lytton appeared in the doorway, a book in his hand.

"Oh. Sorry to disturb. Didn't realize anyone was in here."

Rosalind saw the love-stricken look on the face of the girl opposite her. She was so surprised it was a moment before she recovered herself and leapt into the breech. "No. Of course you're not disturbing us." She cast about for her next words. "In fact, you are welcome. We are in desperate need of someone to approve what it is we are going to say on the invitations." She looked at Valerie. Now the girl was trying to so hard to appear disinterested in the handsome young officer that she seemed to sulk. "Don't we need an opinion from one of the gentlemen, Lady Valerie?" Rosalind prodded.

"Yes . . ." Valerie joined the conversation reluctantly. Rosalind wanted to give her a good shaking.

Finally the girl brightened a little and managed to hand the piece of paper she'd been reading to Lytton.

As she did, and he reached for it, their fingers touched. Both drew back as if bitten, and the paper fell to the desk in front of Rosalind. She looked from the adoring face of the girl to the revealing one of the man. *So that's the way the wind blows!* she thought. Valerie loves him and he loves Valerie. *I see!*

It would all be so simple if the war had not taken his arm, for clearly he had Moreland's approval. Rosalind, however, had spent too many hours talking with maimed men during the time she had lived with the army. She realized there was a problem, and unhappily understood its magnitude.

She wondered with a huge inward sigh just what was to be done about it.

Chapter 13

Moreland sat at the desk in the study going over his correspondence. The invitations to the lawn party at Castle Winston had brought a gratifying number of acceptances.

The only refusals had been from Mrs. Cox and her daughters. She wrote, at some length, that, while her husband would be more than happy to attend his function, the females in the family were suffering from putrid throats and would be, lamentably, unable to attend. This last was a bit of information the Viscount felt he could have gone to his grave without, and thanked his God, not for the first time, that he was from that class that merely wrote "regrets" and signed their name!

Preparations for the party were going smoothly, which pleased the Viscount greatly. What his odd staff lacked in numbers, it seemed to make up for in enthusiasm. Everyone had thrown themselves into the project, and it was proceeding at a pace even he, admittedly a particular man, found satisfactory.

Wilson himself had taken to horse to go procure the services of the men needed to supply and roast the pig. Moreland had seen him cantering down the drive on a big bay stallion that had been the late Earl's war horse.

He noted that Wilson had a dashed fine seat for a butler. In fact, he rode excellently for any man. The stallion was fresh and playing up for all he was worth. He was bucking hard, head to the ground and heels to the heavens almost every other stride. When he wasn't bucking, he was pulling fiercely at the bit.

The young butler swayed easily to every effort to unseat him and instantly took back every inch of rein the horse had pulled from him. By the time the pair had disappeared from sight down the drive, there was perfect understanding between them, and they moved smoothly and quietly out of his sight. Moreland thought it rather strange that Wilson could ride so well.

Used to servants like his own Baldwin, who had never put a leg over a horse in his life, Moreland found Wilson's riding ability absolutely startling in a butler.

He'd found a lot that startled him in the staff at Castle Winston, now that he thought of it. The other day he'd met the chambermaid they called Ann, or was it Andy?—odd, Andy for a female—coming out of his room. Instead of standing aside for him as was expected from a servant, she had brushed by him with a haughty glance of such chilling reproach that he'd been left standing there, sure he'd just committed an unforgivable breech of manners!

All in all, though they served him well, he was increasingly disturbed about his staff. Especially his very attractive housekeeper.

He raised his head, giving up the pretense of correspondence. Was he beginning to think of *her* in some special way? What the devil was going on in his mind that his thoughts of his housekeeper seemed to come with quotation marks around the pronouns associated with *her*. Damnation. There it was again, that slight hesitation before the *her*. His teeth grated as he saw to it that it didn't happen in his last thought. Very well, now that he was aware of doing it, he would cease!

Such a stupid frustration. If she had been a lady, he'd have known her name. Indeed, he'd have heard it on the lips of the bucks of every club long before he met her.

But servants preserved a peculiar dignity. It was Mrs. Rose and Mr. Wilson even when they were alone belowstairs, and for a male employer to ask a female's Christian name was a breech of etiquette a gentleman did not commit.

He rose from his desk and went to look out the window.

Staring unseeingly at the magnificent view of the Channel, he squared his broad shoulders, widened his stance, and clasped his hands at the small of his back. A soldier at ease.

Moreland, however, was finding no ease in the turmoil of thoughts that besieged his mind.

Good God! Could he be developing a *tendre* for his housekeeper? Impossible! Inconceivable. It simply was not done! He had responsibilities to his ancient name that precluded such a thought. Mrs. Rose . . . He heard his own teeth grate again. Blast it! What was the woman's Christian name? He could hardly be having such a confusion of feelings over a woman whose first name he didn't even know!

And what if he was developing a passion for the woman? She had never given him the slightest sign that she would be open to a discreet arrangement. No, dammit, she behaved at all times with a propriety that was fast going to become, he feared, the bane of his existence.

Still not truly seeing what his eyes beheld on the other side of the window glass, he sighed a great sigh. He might stand there the rest of the day and into the night in the stance of a soldier at ease, but he was finding no ease at all from the battle taking place in his mind.

Meanwhile, at that very moment, Rosalind, Andromeda, and Perseus were holding a council of war in the kitchen.

Perseus wore a frown that had nothing to do with concentration. "What if someone should come who would recognize you, Rosalind?"

"I have been worrying about that for the past few days, myself."

"Perhaps you could be ill that day." Andromeda sounded hopeful.

Rosalind smiled at her. "I'm afraid that is going to have to be the case. I hope I have everything all settled so that things will go smoothly for you without me."

"Great Scot!" Perseus burst out. "You already have them organized to a fare-thee-well, Roz. What more can you possibly do?"

Andromeda added her support. "Just pretend to be ill the evening before." She brought up the next subject cautiously. "Your father hasn't responded to his invitation, but we feel certain he will, and will come, so you have no choice but to play least-in-sight while he is here."

"You believe he will come . . ." Rosalind's voice trailed away. She was so possessed of a poignant desire to be reunited with her father, so longing to see him again that . . . It was impossible, of course. Her father was a man careful of his honor, and he had ordered her out of his life. There was no way he would let her return, she knew.

"Roz, don't tear yourself up about it. He's not lonely, you know. Old Bitwell is with him there at Summerfields more often than not."

"I never cared for Bitwell."

Andromeda and Perseus exchanged looks, suppressing merriment.

Rosalind caught their mood with a laugh and added, "Obviously!"

Her in-laws laughed with her. "Well, we can't but be glad, for otherwise you would have married him instead of Hermes," Perseus said.

"Yes, and then to whom should we turn to make us into proper servants?" Andromeda grinned.

Moreland stood before the pier glass in his dressing room, waiting for Gates to finish tying his cravat. He wanted to fidget. Finally he said, "I wish I could shake this feeling that I have met this housekeeper before, Gates. It is driving me to distraction."

Gates was utterly still for a moment, his hands frozen in their position of tying Moreland's neck-cloth. Then he answered blandly as he resumed his task, "Now, where would a Viscount meet a house-keeper?" As always, he dispensed with the *Your Lordship*, since they were alone. Moreland valued his friendship more than his servitude.

"Nowhere, of course," Moreland answered vaguely, frowning. "It must be simply that she reminds me of someone I have met." He scowled at his reflection in the glass. "Crush the fold under my chin a bit lower," he ordered. "I'll need to see my plate."

Unperturbed, Gates crushed the snowy-white linen in question. "Perhaps someone you met while in the army?"

"No." The Viscount scowled as he ran over in his mind the names and faces of people he had met at his one-duty station. "My army career was lamentably short thanks to that wound I received during my first battle." His voice was a neat balance between bitterness and wry humor.

"Yes, but you . . ." Gates's plans to lead his employer's thoughts away from his personal defeat at Coruña to remembering another time around another campfire near Ciudad Rodrigo the next year were not to be. There was a sharp knock on the door, and Wilson opened it and bowed. "There has been a fire in the kitchen, Your Lordship," he announced, "and Cook says dinner must be put back an hour."

"I'll come!" Moreland's words were clipped, his voice harsh. Gates glanced at him sharply.

"It's all right, Your Lordship. Everything is under control." Wilson's voice held both reassurance and resentment.

Moreland looked at the streak of soot on his butler's smooth forehead, then at his singed eyebrows. "If you don't mind, I shall see for myself."

Wilson stiffened. "Of course, Your Lordship," he said woodenly.

Gates looked on with interest. Did the pup take it as an indication that Moreland didn't trust him to have seen to the problem? Well, it was obvious that Moreland was going to let him. He would hardly confess that he had to make sure his housekeeper was all right. Gates watched as the Viscount ran to the stairs and lightly down them.

With any luck at all, someday the housekeeper would bend over a fire of some sort in his presence and Moreland's memory would be jolted. Until then, Gates decided, he personally was going to leave well-enough alone!

Half an hour earlier Mrs. Green had erupted into the kitchen like a madwoman. Mrs. Freep was trying to calm her. "There, there, Mrs. Green. What can we do for you."

"Wanna see me boys, I do." Her voice was a drunken slur, and she leaned heavily on the staff she carried, her head thrust forward to keep her balance. "An' I ain't gonna be kept from them by the likes o' you."

Castor saw the signal Cook made behind the woman's back. Hesitating only long enough to pick up his skirt—it was his turn to be the scullery maid—he fled to find Perseus.

Bursting into the dining room, he blurted, "Come quick! Mrs. Green's drunk and ugly in the kitchen!"

"Damn." Perseus dropped the napkins and started after his brother.

"Wait. I'll come, too." Rosalind placed her handful of silverware carefully on the table and hurried after them.

In the kitchen, Mrs. Green had tired of Cook's talking. She wanted action. In her present state she didn't particularly care what kind of action, as long as something was going on. Lunging upright, she swung her staff at Cook.

Cook, for all her bulk, was agile enough to avoid the heavy stick, and the blow fell instead on the spit full of game hens Cook had been tenderly basting.

Over went the pot of butter. Into the fire went the sputtering fowl. With a gleeful cackle, Mrs. Green grabbed the twig broom that stood beside the hearth ready to sweep back ashes and threw it into the flames. The dry twigs caught with a *whooosh* when they came in contact with the blaze furnished by the pot of butter. Flames shot from the huge cooking-fireplace. Shadows danced in the kitchen from the sudden flare-up.

Mrs. Green cackled in satisfaction. Cook dragged the laughing woman back from harm. And Perseus burst into the room just in time to see the herbs hanging over the fireplace to dry ignite.

"Holy God!" he exclaimed, only half in prayer.

"Oh, my dear!" Rosalind rushed forward behind him, seizing a bowl of flowers from the table. As Cook fought with Mrs. Green to keep her from throwing the kitchen towel into the conflagration, Perseus beat out the flames under the mantelpiece, heady scents of rosemary and thyme swirling about him. Rosalind yanked the flowers from their bowl and poured the water onto the flames. It was all over in those few minutes.

"Whew." Perseus drew a sleeve across his heated brow leaving a black trail of soot. "That was close."

"Indeed it was!" Miss Evans, who had been ready to help but stood back and watched proudly as Perseus charged in, couldn't have agreed more.

Cook glared at Mrs. Green. "What in heaven's name were you thinking of, Mrs. Green? Have you taken leave of your senses?"

Rosalind was bending gracefully over the destruction of the game hens. "Perseus, tell them we must put dinner back an hour."

"Done." Perseus left the kitchen at a run. Dealing with fires was one thing. Dealing with the ominous Mrs. Freep and the unrepentant Mrs. Green was quite another. He was more than willing to leave that to Rosalind!

Peace reigned in the kitchen for a few minutes as Rosalind took a long-handled fork and raked the game birds out of the fireplace. "I think we can yet fix something for dinner using the meat of these, Cook," she said pensively.

Mrs. Green drew herself unsteadily to her full height. Straggling gray hair awry from her tussle with Cook, she glared at her nemesis. "Fix? I'll fix you, Elvira Freep!"

The two older women stood stock still. A long moment of animosity crackled between them. Rosalind, unaware of their tension in her concern for the necessity to provide dinner, reached for the platter warming in its rack beside the fireplace. She straightened from the hearth, the game birds safe on the serving plate, "I think we can . . ." At that moment Mrs. Green's staff, swung with no more than drunken force, and, unfortunately for the unsuspecting Rosalind with drunken error, connected with the side of Rosalind's head.

"No!" Moreland's mighty shout thundered through the kitchen as he leapt into it, ignoring the short flight of stairs. "No!" he cried again as he dashed across the room to where Rosalind lay crumpled on the hearth and Mrs. Green was preparing to remedy her error by taking another swing at Cook.

Mrs. Green took one look at the blazing fury in this madman's eyes and fled out the back door. Cook stood with her eyes as round as dinner plates and her mouth shaped to a soundless "Oh."

Moreland was beside her in that instant. He swooped Rosalind up in his arms and headed for the stairs. "Don't just stand there gaping, Cook! Go fetch my sister. Hurry!"

Mrs. Freep moved faster than she had moved in many a year, lumbering up the short flight of steps in his wake like a charging elephant. As Moreland carried Rosalind with infinite care into the morning room, the corpulent cook panted past him and pounded toward the stairs.

Moreland laid Rosalind carefully on the settee and looked anxiously at her still face. She was so pale. Already a blue bruise was showing on the almost transparent skin along the side of her face. Her eyes were closed, and he saw that her eyelids were faintly tinged with lavender, her long dark lashes tipped with gold.

She was so lovely. Without thought he leaned forward and brushed her lips with his own.

"My God, Moreland," he snarled at himself instantly. "Are you become a lecher? Or do you fancy yourself in the role of Prince Charming?" His chest was tight with the storm of emotion that filled him. Never had he offered offense to a servant. What in Hades was he thinking of?

He settled back on his heels, his mouth set in a grim line and his brow furrowed. Even as he watched, striving not to gaze hungrily into her face, her eyelids fluttered.

The cook hurried into the room. "She's coming," Mrs. Freep reported in a wheezing gasp. Then, seeing Rosalind dazedly opening her eyes, she cried without thinking, "Oh, milady! I am so glad that you are . . ." She stopped, appalled at giving away the well-kept secret of Rosalind's identity! As she struggled with the confusion that assailed her at her unthinking betrayal of them all, Lady Valerie rushed into the room. Cook took a deep, shaking, *terribly* grateful breath and said, ". . . that you are here so quickly!" She turned pointedly to the blond beauty that hurried to Moreland's side.

Valerie knelt beside her brother in one fluid movement. "Oh, dear! What has befallen Mrs. Rose?"

"Some madwoman in the kitchen struck her down."

"How can that be?" Valerie pulled her dressing gown more closely around her and stared wide-eyed at her brother.

"I don't know, but you may rest assured that I intend to find out." The Viscount's voice was a menacing growl.

Mrs. Freep felt that this was the perfect moment to return to her proper place in the kitchen. After all, Lady Rosalind was beginning to struggle to sit up—something the master was determined she was not going to do, and dinner had to be ready in an hour. With surprising stealth for one of her size, she made good her escape.

Rosalind murmured, "Ummmm," and pressed her hand to her forehead. Moreland looked at his sister a little wildly.

Valerie offered, "I'll go get my vinaigrette."

Moreland nodded curtly, and she rose and hurried out of the morning room. Rosalind saw the grim set to the Viscount's face. "Please," she said weakly. "There is no need to be so concerned. I am fine." She pushed his restraining hand gently away and sat up. Speaking more firmly, she said, "I am all right, truly. It is no worse than a spill from my horse, I assure you."

Moreland growled, "People have been killed falling from horses." Concern roughened his voice.

Rosalind's heart leapt to hear it. "Truly, I am fine. Mrs. Green wasn't trying to hurt me, you know. In fact"—she gave a gurgle of laughter, wincing—"I think she was aiming at Cook."

Moreland's eyes, on a level with her own as he knelt before her, filled with admiration, and Rosalind's head spun seeing it.

"You are certain you have no ill effects?"

"None but the assault on my dignity and a few

ashes on my skirt," she said gently, her gray eyes full of tenderness.

"I . . ." Somehow he got lost in the contemplation of her eyes and forgot what he wanted to say. He cleared his throat and was about to try to begin again when his sister hurried into the room, her vinaigrette in her hand.

She stared at her brother kneeling before the seated housekeeper. "Here it is, but I don't suppose you need it now," she said sharply.

Moreland rose easily. "No, Mrs. Rose is recovered."

"Good." Valerie turned on her heel and stalked out.

Moreland watched her go with a frown. "You must forgive my sister. I don't know what has come over her lately."

Rosalind was startled into saying, "Do you not?"

Moreland stared at her. "And you do." His tone was dry.

Rosalind had the grace to blush.

Moreland, his feelings outraged by his reaction to this woman, retreated behind his station in life. He demanded haughtily, "Suppose you explain to me what ails my sister. After all, you have known her so long and so intimately."

Stung, she shot to her feet at his scorn, pushing his steadying hand away even as she swayed. The man was certainly one of many moods! Hotly she told him, "Any ninny could see that she is in love with the lieutenant. And any ninny could see that he is too *noble*"—she weighted her words with sarcasm—"to *tie her to a cripple*. No wonder the poor child is so unhappy!"

Moreland all but flinched under the lash of her scorn.

Rosalind, her feelings already lacerated by the hopelessness of her present position, had not needed this treatment. She was heedless. "Men! They know nothing, see nothing!" she muttered savagely. So why did she have to find this one so . . .

She slammed a mental door on the thought, turned a disdainful shoulder to Moreland, and, like Valerie, stalked out. Only, due to a slight dizziness, it was not done half so well.

Chapter 14

Rosalind literally fell into her bed that night, her head still aching from the blow Mrs. Green had erroneously struck her. The excitement in the kitchen had left her exhausted, and her quarrel with Moreland had so ravaged her emotions that she refused to think of him.

She forced her mind to safer thoughts. She was utterly weary from bending over the desk in the study all day writing lists of duties, supplies, games, and equipment for the party without any activity to relieve and rejuvenate her. In addition, in the back of her mind she kept returning, like a terrier worrying a rat, to the problem of unrequited love she had discovered when she and Valerie were writing the invitations.

That it was unnecessary for the love to *be* unrequited was a frustration she was finding hard to bear. Flinging her frustration into Moreland's teeth hadn't made it any easier, either. She tried to put it all out of her mind.

She was lying there waiting for sleep to come and massaging the cramp in her overused right hand when she heard a muffled sound.

Shooting bolt upright in her bed, she identified a soft sobbing just outside her door. Sliding from the edge of her high four-poster, she ran to the door and yanked it open.

Cassie stood just outside, tears streaming down her face. "Oh, Rosalind. I was trying to decide whether or not to disturb you. I'm so sorry!" With an obvious effort she stopped crying.

"Disturb me about what, dearest?" She put an arm comfortingly around the girl and pulled her into the room. "What is it that has so upset you?"

"My mare, Queen of Hearts." She gulped back a sob and tried not to cry. "She's in foal to Hermes's charger, you know."

"Yes?"

"Well, her time has come. Only something must be wrong. One of the stableboys tossed pebbles at my window and told me if . . ." Cassie began to sob again. ". . . if I wanted to see her one last time, I should come." She clutched Rosalind's hand. "Oh, Roz. There is so little left of our old lives, and I do love her so. I don't think I can bear it!"

Rosalind ran to the armoire and pulled down two cloaks. Her own she threw about Cassie's shoulders. The other one, which had been Hermes's campaign cloak, she wrapped around herself as she thrust her feet into a pair of half boots. "Come, Cassie. We shall go together, and not just to say good-bye to your mare, either. Surely there is something to be done. If nothing else, our prayers and your presence will ease her."

The two slipped through the darkened house. After first lighting a lantern from those hanging on the kitchen wall near the back door, they left the house and hurried quietly down the path leading to the stables.

Once there, Cassie broke into a run, calling, "Queenie! Here I am!"

Rosalind followed her to a stall where an attractive chestnut mare lay sprawled in the fresh straw, tossing her head and moaning. Sweat covered her, and the spasms that should have produced her foal quivered over her abdomen.

MacFie and Gates, the Viscount's valet, crouched over the mare's hindquarters while the head groom smoothed a consoling hand along her satiny chestnut neck.

Cassie pushed into the stall and went to the mare's head. There she sank down on the straw and lifted the mare's head into her lap. Stroking the prostrate animal's brow, she let silent tears rain down.

Rosalind demanded, "Is there nothing to be done?"

"The foal is not positioned right." MacFie shook his head at her, not wanting to put into words the hopelessness of the situation.

"Surely we can do *something*!"

Gates turned to look at her. Rosalind liked him; he had proved to be no problem at all for the peculiar staff of the castle. He hung with MacFie, spoke little, and regarded them with amused eyes that seemed to know exactly what they were up to and to promise he would never tell.

Rosalind had the vague feeling she had seen him before, but had no time to give the matter thought just now. He explained to her, "If we break the sac the little one is in before we get his head, he may die."

"Have you tried?" Rosalind's voice held a note of urgency. While she had not been exposed to a great deal of her father's horse breeding, she was at least aware that mares, unlike their human counterparts, delivered their babies in well under half an hour, and were in trouble if they didn't.

"With our arms so big, it's hard to feel where the limbs are"—he sighed heavily—"and we fear to injure the mare."

Cassie sobbed.

Rosalind looked at the brawny arms of the two heavily built men and moved to kneel between the men in the straw at the mare's rump. "Here," she said quietly, ignoring the horrified faces of the men and rolling up the sleeves of her nightrail, "let me."

Moreland was restless. Again and again he relived the scene in the kitchen. Suppose he hadn't decided to go down to be sure the fire was out? Suppose the madwoman had struck the housekeeper—damn! He still didn't know her name!—again? And again? It didn't bear thinking on.

He'd torn his sheets loose and balled up his comforter. Having made a battlefield of his bed tossing and turning, now he couldn't rest in the resultant mess. His thoughts made sleep impossible anyway. With a heavy sigh he rose and slipped his banian on. As he did, he chanced to glance out the window and watched a light move from the house to the stable yard.

"Now, what the devil?" he demanded. Tossing his banian from him, he started instead to struggle into breeches and boots. "What the deuce is happening in my stables?"

Moreland moved silently into the area just beyond the light when he reached the barn. A moment later, seeing what was transpiring, he opened the half door and joined, unnoticed behind Gates and MacFie, the crowd in the commodious foaling stall.

His housekeeper, her slender arm thrust into the mare, was saying, "The legs are both bent so that the knees are forward, and the head is turned backward!" Her eyes were wide and beseeching as she looked toward the men. "Does that mean it is hopeless?"

Gates said, "Not if we are able to turn his head and straighten his legs. It must be hooves first and his head between them. But our arms are still too brawny, and that may be beyond your strength."

"But not beyond mine." Moreland stepped forward to a chorus of surprised comments.

Cassie was the first to recover. "Oh, would you, Your Lordship? I should be eternally grateful," she said with heartfelt warmth, then caught herself and added rather lamely, "if I were the Miss Winston who owned the mare."

Rosalind said, "Best sent for Pers . . . er, Mr. Wilson, MacFie. He, too, is of a less brawny build than you and Mr. Gates."

"Aye, Mrs. Rose. I'll rouse the lad in case we have need of him."

Moreland moved to stand beside Rosalind. She tried to rise to give him her place, but she had been sitting on her legs too long, and they refused to obey her order to rise. She smiled up at him helplessly. He understood her dilemma without explanation and reached down to her, lifting her effortlessly to her feet.

She felt herself blush. She knew she must not only look a fright, but must also present an appearance that her employer could only consider scandalous.

Moreland took his hands from her and stood staring down at her. Standing there with one blood-streaked arm, and the other clad only in the light lawn of her lace-trimmed nightgown—standing in the voluminous folds of a battle-stained warrior's cloak—his housekeeper touched a chord within him that had long lain silent. Now it rang through him, clamoring for him to remember. But try as he might, he could not. What had blood and battle to do with this beautiful woman who so fascinated him?

Suddenly two more people joined their little band with a clatter that startled the mare and broke the spell under which the Viscount labored.

"Better get Pers!"

"Right away!" And half the whirlwind spun back out into the dark night before anyone could tell him MacFie had already gone.

As he knelt slowly in the straw behind the mare, Moreland saw the white face of his page, the boy barely tall enough to be seen over the half door.

Blush gone with the work at hand, Rosalind sank down beside him and explained in a whisper what she'd discovered about the foal's position in the dam's womb.

Moreland rolled up his own sleeves and washed arms and hands in the bowl of soapy water Gates offered.

With his housekeep giving low-voiced comments, he began to straighten the first foreleg. The mare moaned and thrashed, shoving Mrs. Rose into him. With complete calm she righted herself and continued to watch him.

He glanced up and saw her lips moving as if in prayer, but her eyes never left his arm. Sweat broke out on his forehead as he strained to move the sharp little hoof of the second foreleg without doing any damage.

Rosalind saw the perspiration on the Viscount's forehead and wiped it away with the clean sleeve of her nightrail, smiling apologetically.

Moreland smiled his gratitude but dared not break his concentration to speak. The second foreleg was in the proper position now, and he sat back on his heels to rest before he tackled the head.

Rosalind smiled at him encouragingly. "You are doing wonderfully."

He smiled down at her where she sat, now, in the straw beside him. "You did the difficult part. You discovered . . . uhmm . . . the lay of the land, so to speak."

She smiled gently at his gallant attempt at discretion. "But I hadn't the strength to right things."

"We're not through it yet, you know."

Cassie's eyes got even wider, but she didn't begin

to cry again. She just watched the two at her horse's hindquarters unwaveringly and kept praying and stroking her mare's forehead.

Perseus arrived looking anything but the proper butler, Wilson, his hair much disarranged by sleep. Two pages, where Moreland was certain there should only be one, stood with him at the half-door.

Wilson said, "Tell me what you want me to do when you want me, sir." In his concern, titles were forgotten.

Moreland signified he'd heard with a nod and, after rewashing his hand, began to try to turn the foal's head. The mare moaned but didn't thrash this time. Moreland strained mightily, sinews in his neck standing out as the muscles in his arm and back bulged and rippled under the fine linen of his shirt.

Eyes closed and jaw clenched, he made one more herculean effort, shifting his right leg forward so that he could better his position by digging in with the heel of his boot.

The mare grunted. The Viscount continued his pull, and the nose slid into place between the two front feet. He threw a glance over his shoulder at Gates. "Help me," he gasped. The big man leapt to a position beside Moreland and closed his own hands around Moreland's arm like a vise. As a team, they continued to pull, Moreland concentrating only on keeping his grip, relying on the larger man to supply the strength of the pull, until the tiny hooves, then the forelegs, then the nose, head, neck, and finally the shoulders of the foal appeared.

There was a very subdued cheer from the three at the half-door, and a grateful sob of relief from

Cassie at the mare's head. An instant later they were all leaping for safety, as the back half of the foal was born and the mare struggled to her feet.

Suddenly the stall was too small for all those in it, and Moreland put an arm around Rosalind's waist to usher her out. Cassie stayed behind with the head groom making wonderful crooning sounds of endearment and comfort as the mare anxiously watched the groom check her baby.

"A fine colt, Your Lordship!"

Moreland was looking down into Rosalind's face, savoring the rapport they shared, and so missed the triumphant look on that of his butler when he heard the head groom's announcement.

Nevertheless, when he finally returned to his battlefield of a bed, he had the strangest feeling that the head groom had not been speaking to him when he'd said *Your Lordship!*

Chapter 15

Rosalind did pretend to be ill on the day of the lawn party. Nothing less than the threat of being recognized by her father could have induced her to keep from her duties, and even then she felt guilty.

Unable to stay in her room, she climbed to the battlements. She wanted just one glimpse of the austere Earl of Summerfield before the day was out.

While Rosalind made her way to the parapet atop the castle, Lytton stood beside Moreland on the terrace overlooking the great sweep of lawn on the leeward side of the huge edifice. "It looks as if everything is going well, Edward."

"Indeed." Moreland looked out over the considerable crowd of neighbors who had come in response to the invitations Rosalind and Lady Valerie had labored over so faithfully only days before. His guests had joined in the lighthearted spirit of a casual picnic with good humor.

Even Valerie seemed to be enjoying the festivities.

"I have quite forgiven you for having a lawn party instead of a ball, Edward," she said, smiling up from under the wide brim of her leghorn hat. "This beautiful day has saved you."

She turned to her brother's companion, and her expression became intense, her words sharp in spite of the lightness of her comment. "As for you, Harry, I can only reprimand you for wearing your uniform. You will break all the young ladies' hearts." Her last words were spoken so cuttingly that her brother was startled. For a brief instant he wondered if there was something to his housekeeper's remark about Valerie and Harry Lytton.

At that moment, a woman in an outrageous fruit-and flower-laden hat bustled up with some agitation. She demanded that Valerie take her inside at once to see again the portrait of the late Earl of Winston. Valerie acceded to the woman's request as graciously as a duchess.

"What the devil got into her?" Moreland asked Lytton as Valerie left them to escort the lady into the house to see the portrait of the late Earl of Winston.

Lytton was staring after Valerie and didn't answer for a moment. When he did, it was with an obvious change of subject. "She evidently wants to see a portrait."

"Not her. Valerie. She has suffered a drastic change of personality since she was presented. I'm at a loss to know how to handle the chit."

Color flooded Lytton's cheeks and receded, leaving him pale under his sun-bronzed skin. "She seems to have taken offense to my wearing my uniform. Remind me to write Weston and see where my new clothes are, won't you?" Lytton's voice was so colorless, his friend stared at him for a long moment.

When Moreland finally spoke again, it was on a new topic. "From the report Attleborough sent, I think the men who are of most interest to us are the two by that large oak."

Lytton nodded.

Moreland and Lytton strolled across the lawn to the men in question. "Are you enjoying the day, gentlemen?" Moreland smiled and watched both carefully without seeming to show more than a host's casual interest in his guests.

Lord Alton cleared his throat and said, "These country entertainments do very well for just what you intended. We are certainly all together, and quickly, too. Fine idea to put this on and give us the chance to look you over right away."

Moreland, more amused than taken aback by the man's plain speaking, smilingly murmured, "So glad you approve."

Lieutenant Lytton bowed his close-cropped blond head and coughed into his hand.

Alton's companion laughed and reassured his host, "You may be sure he likes it, Your Lordship. If there is one thing you may count upon with our Lord Alton, it is that he will plainly speak his mind!"

"You're Radley, if I'm not mistaken." Moreland extended his hand.

"I am indeed! And very pleased to meet you." Radley clasped the Viscount's hand and wrung it heartily. The process was repeated with Lytton, and a conversation followed involving the party, the weather, and the number of neighbors present.

Radley had just mentioned Lady Valerie and his desire to call on her if Moreland would permit it, when two older gentlemen marched up much in the manner of a frontal assault.

Radley said, "Ah, here is another of your neighbors, and his very distinguished friend. May I have the honor of introducing you to the Earl of Summerfield"—the Earl bowed briefly—"and General Bitwell?"

Moreland, his guests thus identified for him, bid them welcome.

High above them on the rampart of the castle, Rosalind hid behind one of the merlons, clutching her cloak against the sharp wind that cut across the roof from the sea. Holding wind-whipped tendrils of hair back out of her eyes, she peered down around the smooth stone behind which she huddled striving for one glimpse of her father. Her heart leapt when she saw him as he approached Moreland.

She followed her father with her eyes as he mingled with the other guests. He stayed the better part of the day, quietly enjoying being among his neighbors, in spite of his friend's impatient aloofness.

On the battlement, Rosalind gathered her cloak closer around her and wished, not for the first time, that she had worn Hermes's heavier one. Below her, finally, even the sun-warmed, castle-sheltered lawn began to chill, and her father, and many others, gathered around Moreland to give him their thanks and their farewells.

Rosalind watched her father as he walked sedately to his waiting coach, then watched the vehicle until she could see it no more. By then she was thoroughly chilled, and the tears that marked her smooth cheeks were icy.

With a heavy heart she crossed the roof to the stone stairs that led down into the castle. As she began to descend, she was shaken by so mighty a sneeze that she nearly lost her footing. She avoided a serious fall only by clutching the handrail some thoughtful Winston had added to the treacherous, curving stairs not many generations ago. Reluctant to meet any of the family while she was feeling so forlorn, she went straight to her room.

The cheerful fire on her hearth failed to warm her. She went to her mirror and studied the pale face with the wind-reddened cheeks she saw there. "Well, milady. I think if you don't want to have a nasty cold, it behooves you to crawl into your bed and nurse some warmth back into your bones." She smiled at her reflection as if she had spoken to an old friend, but even as she did, she had to admit that she was putting herself to bed as much to avoid people as to get warm. It simply wouldn't do to let her friends see her when her mood was so low.

At dinner, Moreland, Lady Valerie, and Lytton, worn out by their success, discussed at length the events of the day. Lady Valerie was more animated than Moreland had seen her since her come-out.

At the first lull in their conversation, "Who in the world was the strange lady who dragged you off into the castle, Val?" Moreland wanted to know.

Valerie laughed and frowned at the same time. "That was Lady Webster. She had been staring at poor Wilson all the time he was on the lawn and was certain he must be related to the late Earl. She insisted on showing me the Earl's portrait as proof she was right."

Moreland glanced over his shoulder at Wilson. The boy butler had washed from his hair the heavy oil with which he had plastered it to his head for the lawn party. His head was again its usual mass of dark curls as he performed his duties calmly and competently, his cheeks aflame. Moreland looked at him speculatively. Himself a master of disguise, he wondered if the oily hair was not simply a method to remain of neat appearance on a windy day. Perhaps he would have a look at the portrait of the Earl of Winston, himself.

Moreland changed the subject. "The soup is unusually good this evening, don't you think, Val?"

"Yes. I can't imagine where the Winstons found such a marvelous cook so far from London."

"Wherever, I for one am most grateful," Lytton said.

"Yes, my friend. You of all of us have need of good food to put some meat back on your bones."

It was Lytton's turn to be embarrassed. "Yes, well, I was somewhat ill. . . ."

"Oh, for pity's sake! You nearly died!" Half rising from her chair with a hand at her slender throat, Valerie didn't merely speak, she raged at him. "You came back half dead with an awful wound." Tears filled her eyes. "You wouldn't let your friends near you to care for you." The tears spilled over and ran down her cheeks. "Then you lost your arm and have been moping ever since. It's no wonder you need fattening like a lamb for slaughter when you refused to let *anyone* take care of you!" She rose, the color hectic in her cheeks, threw her napkin on the table—right into the soup her brother had just praised—and stormed from the dining room, blond curls flying.

"My God! What the hell was that all about?" Moreland demanded of no one in particular, half out of his chair as if he would pursue his sister. He saw, in his mind's eye, the disdainful face of his housekeeper.

Lytton, however, didn't answer him but sat as one stunned, the color gone from his face.

Perseus, for his part, gave a tremendous sigh of relief. The moment had passed safely in which he'd been certain Lady Valerie was going to relate Lady Webster's rather memorable reaction to his revelation.

After all, it would hardly reflect well on him as a perfect butler for it to come out that Lady Webster had been more than a little shocked to hear his own blasé assurance that he resembled the late Earl because he was one of his bastards.

Chapter 16

Andromeda visited Rosalind as soon as she saw that her sister-in-law was not present for breakfast at the big pine table in the servants' hall.

"Are you ill, Roz?" Her voice filled with concern, Andromeda closed the door behind her and hastened across the comfortable sitting room. Pausing in the doorway of Rosalind's bedchamber, she saw Rosalind's color was high and worried that it might signal possible fever.

"Oh, dearest, *are* you ill?" Andromeda placed her cool hand on Rosalind's forehead. "You do feel a trifle feverish."

Rosalind smiled at her and said wryly, "If I were ill, it would only serve me right for shirking my duties yesterday by feigning to be."

"Never say so, Roz, for your father did attend the garden party. You did the only thing you could have done under the circumstances."

"Yes. It would have been very painful for us both had we met."

Her voice was so wistful, Andromeda felt compelled to ask, "Do you wish you might have seen him?"

"Oh, but I did see him."

Andromeda's expression asked the question.

"I stood on the roof, hidden behind the parapet." She smiled tremulously at her friend. "Like the true daughter of an old soldier, I stood guard." She smiled and used a soldier's knowledge of battlements in an attempt to amuse her troubled sister-in-law. "I crouched behind my merlon and stared down through my crenel all day long." Her smile became determinedly brighter. "I did get to see my father."

Andromeda heard the longing in Rosalind's voice and could think of nothing to say. After a moment, she asked softly, "Was it longing to speak with him that gave you a sleepless night?" She reached out a gentle index finger and lightly touched the dark smudges under Rosalind's eyes.

Rosalind found herself confiding to Andromeda. "I wish things could be all right between my father and me, but I fear it is hopeless. When one is as stubborn as my sire, there is not much chance of his ever changing his mind, I'm afraid. I daresay I spent as much time sleepless because I was trying to contrive a way to bring Lady Valerie and the Lieutenant together as I did worrying about the rift between Papa and me."

Andromeda's face showed her concern for her friend's grief briefly, then lit up like an urchin's in a candy shop. "Is there something between the Lieutenant and Moreland's sister?"

"Watch them and you will see." Rosalind smiled. "Though the Viscount seemed unaware of it, the attachment is as plain as the nose on his face."

"Perhaps I could help things along." Andromeda's eyes took on a faraway look.

"I think it would be best . . . Ah-choo! . . . if you just left things well enough alone." Rosalind looked at Andromeda earnestly over her lace-edged handkerchief.

"You are truly coming down with a cold, *ma belle soeur*. I think you had probably better remain in your bed for the rest of the day at least."

"Andromeda!" Rosalind's voice was menacing. Not for a moment was she distracted by the girl's sudden concern for her health. "What are you thinking of doing?"

"Nothing, dearest," Andromeda said airily. "But I must go now." She put on a serious face. "I have my duties, you know."

With a quick peck in the direction of Rosalind's cheek, she slipped away and out of the housekeeper's quarters, leaving Rosalind to fervently hope that Andromeda would not do anything that the whole household might regret.

Moreland, having plowed through most of his correspondence, demanded of Perseus, "Wilson, have you seen Mrs. Rose this morning?"

Perseus took one look at the dark scowl on the Viscount's face and grinned inside. "No, Your Lordship. I believe she is in her bed, ill."

"Ill! Why was I not told?" Moreland advanced on

Perseus as if he would shake information out of his butler.

Perseus bravely stood his ground. "It is only a cold, Your Lordship."

Moreland glared at him, then spun on his heel and stalked off.

"Phew!" was all Perseus allowed himself to say, but his speculations were considerably more lengthy.

Lady Valerie looked up from her embroidery as her brother erupted into the morning room. "Whatever has gotten into you, Edward?"

"Go and see how ill Mrs. Rose is," he ordered her.

"I *beg* your pardon!" Valerie's temper, a faculty she had only lately become aware she possessed, flared at his attitude. Before she could form a further comment, her brother went on.

"Wilson tells me she is ill. I can hardly go and see for myself!" He raked a hand distractedly through his neatly combed hair, all the while towering over her.

She dropped her embroidery and rose, shoving her hand against his chest to move him back far enough for her to stand comfortably. "Edward Forsythe, what in heaven's name has gotten into you?" She stamped her tiny foot at him.

"It's common decency to be concerned about the health of one's staff, Valerie," he informed her in frigid tones.

"Ha!" She shook her finger under his nose. "I don't recall you ripping me away from my own pursuits to send me flying to Fridley's bedside when *he* was indisposed!"

"Fridley wasn't a delicate woman." Moreland

fought his agitation. "And we had plenty of servants to see to him. Mrs. Rose is a vital part of a very meager staff here." He glared self-righteously at his sister. "Her well-being impacts on our own comfort." He tried to stare her down.

Valerie was having none of it. She knew her brother too well. She said with ponderous dignity, "Very well, I shall go to see Mrs. Rose." She didn't voice it, but her whole attitude said that he would now owe her a favor in return for her compliance.

Clenching his teeth, he followed her from the morning room. They ascended the grand staircase to the spacious landing. The quarters for housekeeper and butler opened off opposite ends of the very large landing. Moreland stood at the window, pretending to look at the view, as Valerie raised her hand to tap at the door.

Before she could do more, the door opened, and the chambermaid, Ann, came out. There was a scowl of fierce concentration on her face that did nothing to quiet the Viscount's fears.

Startled to see the Viscount and his sister, Andy dropped a quick curtsy and started to move away, intent on her plan to talk to Harry Lytton.

Valerie stopped her with a question. "Have you been seeing to Mrs. Rose? Is she seriously unwell?"

Completely forgetting her role as chambermaid, Lady Andromeda looked at the Forsythe girl for the first time with eyes that held sympathy. After all, if Roz was right, the poor girl was suffering the pangs of a love that did not run smoothly. "It is only a cold, dear," she graciously reassured her, gently patting her arm. "She'll be fine by tomorrow, I'm certain." So saying, she nodded regally to the

Viscount and left them both standing there, Valerie open-mouthed and astounded, as she left to go about her duties.

Moreland looked at his astonished sister, laughter lightening his mood. "Yes," he said kindly. "It is precisely the same with me. I keep getting the distinct impression that the servants here graciously consider me an equal."

Valerie stared at him incredulously for a moment, then confided, "You know, Edward, I had the oddest thing happen yesterday and today. Yestereve, I asked the page to run out to the folly beside the lake and bring me a book I had been reading there and had forgotten."

"And?"

"And I did not get it until this morning, when the *scullery maid*, of all things, ran up to me on my way down to breakfast and thrust it into my hand with a breathless apology for not giving it to me last evening. Whatever do you make of that?"

"I make of it, dearest sister, that we have a most unusual staff here at Castle Winston. You must not trouble yourself about it."

Valerie blinked, started to speak, and closed her mouth.

Moreland merely smiled at her. He was too interested to see how the game would play out to its end to enlighten his sister and perhaps have her spoil it.

Valerie frowned at him a long moment, then gave up. She knew her brother too well to suppose he would tell her anything before it suited him.

Finally she gave an irritated shrug and turned away to rap once sharply upon the door before which they stood. Hearing a sound that could not be distinguished from a sneeze, she opened the door and, leaving her anxious brother to cool his heels at the great window on the marble landing, went in and closed it behind her.

Lytton sat at the desk in the study where he had gone to look over the reports from the men he and Moreland had in their scanty command, and stared at the note in his hand. "Who the devil wants to meet me on the beach?" He turned the note over, but the back held no more clue to the sender than did the front.

The writing was distinctly that of an educated woman, but if his memory served him right, it was nothing like the housekeeper's, and of course he knew it wasn't Valerie's.

Every stroke and whorl of Valerie's handwriting lived in a special place in his heart, and had since he'd fallen head over heels in love with the minx when she was but fifteen.

It had been Valerie's letters that had amused and sustained him through the last two harrowing years he'd spent in the army. There was no way this imperious command could have come from Valerie.

If not Valerie, and not the housekeeper, then who could be demanding that he meet them on the beach at five-thirty this evening? For a moment he glared at the paper as if by sheer intensity of will he could force it to give up the secret of its sender. Then abruptly he stuffed it into his pocket and strode purposefully out of the house and off in the direction of the path that led down the cliffs toward the sea.

Chapter 17

Moreland was relieved to hear his sister say that Mrs. Rose appeared to be suffering only the slightest of colds. When assured that his housekeeper intended to return to her duties on the morrow, he was finally able to concentrate on the reports he had been studying on the movements of the very brief list of gentlemen he had given his men orders to spy upon.

The reports were not lengthy, as the men had only been on duty two days. He and Lytton thought themselves fortunate they had received the four men they had requested from Attleborough to assist the one man already on watch in the area. That there were four of them assigned to him told Moreland just how seriously the War Office took this particular leakage of information to Napoleon. It was a sobering thought.

Moreland sighed heavily and took up his quill to

report, in his turn, on the reports spread out in front of him.

Valerie was restless. She wasn't at all certain that she liked Moreland's preoccupation with the house-keeper, Mrs. Rose. She liked the woman, so it wasn't that. It was the dreadful *unsuitability* of her brother's seeming regard for her.

Marriage was, of course, out of the question. She and all the rest of the Forsythe family would place heaven and earth in the way of such a match. And if Edward should try to set her up as his mistress, why, then she herself would fight him, for she had come to both like and respect the quiet woman who ran the castle so competently.

Uncomfortable with her thoughts and unable to interest herself in her book, Valerie decided to walk along the cliffs. The exercise and the fresh air would, she hoped, go a long way toward putting her spirits to rights. Calling for her cloak and a pair of walking boots, she left the shelter of the sprawl-ing castle and headed for the cliff tops.

The breeze was brisk off the water, and she found the racks of clouds sailing by particularly spectacu-lar in the low light of the sun.

She walked closer to the edge of the cliff to see if the tide was coming in. Glancing down to the wet shingle she saw that the water was advancing upon the shore steadily with each wave. The tide was indeed coming in.

She lost herself in the fascination of the rhythm of the waves as they swept ashore, then danced away, only to be caught up and hurled back toward the foot of the cliffs by other waves behind them before they could regain the sea.

Suddenly a woman came into her line of sight. She was heavily cloaked against the sea air, and Valerie had no idea who she was. Not so with the man who strode to meet her from the opposite direction! With a gasp Valerie recognized the close-cropped blond hair and the scarlet regimentals. Lytton! *Her* Lytton!

The two stood a moment talking, then the brazen hussy in the dark cloak slipped her arm through Lytton's only one, and they proceeded casually up the beach. Gasping in disbelief, Valerie stared down on them with murder in her heart.

An instant later the desire to do away with the man she loved and the unknown woman was replaced by a very real fear for their safety. The breeze had turned stronger, and now drove the tide before it. It began to look to her as if there were a very real danger of the pair being caught on the beach by the surging tide. They risked being swept out to sea!

Her broken heart forgotten, she ran along the cliff tops calling her warning down to them. It was pointless. Unable to hear her over the noise of the wind and the waves, they continued on at a leisurely pace, unaware of their danger.

Valerie stood, indecisive, for a full minute. Then she ran back the way she had come, going for help to rescue Lytton and the woman before they could be swept away.

Bursting into the house, she called at the top of her lungs, "Wilson! Edward! Come! I need you!"

"What is it?" Rosalind's voice seemed to have caught some of the panic in Valerie's. "What is the matter?"

Valerie looked up the grand staircase. Rosalind, descending from the landing asked, "Has there been an accident?"

"Oh! Thank heavens!" Valerie rushed to meet the housekeeper at the foot of the stairs. "No, there has not been an accident, yet, but there may be one at any moment! Harry and some woman are in immediate danger of being swept out to sea!"

Rosalind looked into the girl's frantic eyes and reached out to her. "Try to be calm and tell me the whole."

"There is nothing more to tell!" Valerie clung to Rosalind's hands as if she grasped a lifeline. "They are walking on the beach, and the wind is rising and driving the tide in faster than I have ever seen it come."

"That could be dangerous indeed." Rosalind, glad she had decided to give up the role of convalescent, whirled and ran toward the door. "I know the beach, and the cliff caves as well." She paused with her hand on the knob. "I'll catch them and try to lead them to safety—one way or the other." Then she was out the door and calling back, "Find the men and follow!"

Valerie hesitated only an instant before dashing off to do the housekeeper's bidding.

Summoned by his frantic sister, Moreland, shoulder to shoulder with Perseus, rushed to the cliff top. Valerie ran behind him, her cloak flying back from her shoulders in the rising wind. "Why the deuce didn't you stop her, Valerie?"

His sister, straining to see any one of the three

people they all knew were on the shingle below them, didn't answer.

Perseus, his own eyes scanning the beach anxiously, said, "Don't worry. She knows the tides and the beach here as well as anyone." He gave them more reassurance than he himself felt. "She'll find a way to get them up or keep them safe."

Moreland growled in frustration. Lytton's safety was of paramount importance to him, and the life of the woman with him must certainly be a concern too, but it was his housekeeper's headlong dash into the danger that had Moreland beside himself. He didn't know what he would do if anything happened to her.

Why the devil was she down there, anyway! She was supposed to be in bed with a cold, not running along a wet beach to save two ninnyhammers who were too stupid to remember the tide!

After what seemed an eon, he saw her below him, running lightly along the beach. Without a moment's hesitation, he tore away from the others and headed for the path down the cliffs.

Forcing his body mercilessly, he ran in pursuit of her slender figure. His long-legged strides ate up the distance between them. With alarm, he saw he would not catch her before the tide reached and swirled around her ankles.

"What in hell are you doing down here!" he shouted at her when he had her arm firmly in his grip.

Startled, she turned wide eyes to him. Their gray echoed the spindrift smoking the Channel in what was rapidly becoming a gale. Her cheeks were wind-whipped to a deep rose. His fingers lost their strength to hold her as his senses staggered under the assault of her beauty.

"I must get to the two people Lady Valerie has seen from atop the cliffs. They may not know the tide is so swift." Determination shone in her eyes.

She had pressed her soft lips almost to his cheek to make him hear over the roar of the waves. Moreland felt as if he'd been hit by lightning. While he stood struck dumb, Rosalind moved ahead. A mighty surge from the Channel rose almost to her hips, staggering her.

Moreland leapt to her side, his arm about her waist in a flash. Hauling her against him, he battled farther up the beach, closer to the cliff base. Looking over his shoulder at the wind-driven sea, he cursed softly and sought a way back to the cliff path. In just the few minutes since he had descended it, the path had been cut off by the seething waves.

He shot a glance upward and saw Valerie, her face a tiny white mask of fear, hugging her cloak tightly around her and staring down at them. Beside her, Perseus was dangerously close to the edge, craning his neck to see a way clear for them. Finally he swung his arm in a broad gesture that Moreland couldn't miss. He pointed in the direction away from the path.

Moreland understood then that escape in that direction was truly cut off. He wasted no time in moving up the beach toward the headland that jutted out into the sea. He hoped that, because it was higher, they might yet cross it safely and attain the broad beach beyond.

Seizing Rosalind's hand, he ran for the tall, forbidding rocks. Rosalind clung to his hand desperately, running as hard as she was able, her wet skirts held clear of her flying feet by her free hand.

The headland seemed forever away! When they reached it, Moreland lifted her to sit on a ledge of rock above the wet strand, and went to discover whether they could safely pass around its point.

As Rosalind waited, she prayed that the people she had come to rescue were safe—but mostly she prayed for the safety of the Viscount. How valiant he was! She could hardly bear to think of how he had put his life at risk.

She looked up eagerly when he appeared back from the point of the headland. Watching the sure manner in which he picked his way over the jumbled rocks, she felt a warmth she couldn't explain. In a moment he was at her side.

Their glances met. His dark-blue eyes looked with deep concern into her lovely gray ones.

Rosalind knew in that instant that they were in mortal peril.

Chapter 18

Rosalind gasped as Moreland caught her firmly around the waist and swung her effortlessly down from her rock perch into water that was now knee-deep. A little tendril of fear stirred as she remembered that when he had lifted her to her seat only a few minutes before, the water had only been ankle high. She fought back the fear as, with a surge of the water, her skirts floated near her hips.

Clinging to his strong hand, she followed him out onto the rocky promontory. Moreland worked his way carefully over the slippery rocks, steadying her as they went.

Time and again they were lashed by spray cast aloft by the crashing waves. Time and again their feet slipped or were almost swept out from under them by the force of the water. The waves pulled at Rosalind and caused her to lose her footing more than once, but Moreland's grip never lessened.

She felt her hair fall free of its pins and trail,

dripping, down to her waist. She had been wishing she had brought her cloak, but now as the weight of her sodden skirts dragged at her every step, she was glad that she had not.

She stumbled and fell heavily in spite of Moreland's help. A fiery burst of pain shot through her as her knee struck the rocks. The blow left her whole leg numb. It felt as if it didn't belong to her. She sobbed in frustration as she tried to command her next step only to have the order refused by her abused limb.

Moreland whipped around and saw her leg buckle under her. Catching her in his arms, he lifted her high against his chest as if she were a child. He struggled on.

Rosalind cried, "No, you must not carry me! You must use your strength to save yourself." She pounded lightly on his shoulder to force him to understand.

"Ballast." He grinned recklessly down into her face. "I am using you for ballast, my dear Mrs. Rose."

Even as her heart turned over at the nearness of his face, handsome as an angel's with its exultant grin, she lost all patience with him. "Do not be foolish. You must hurry to beat the incoming tide up the shoreline! Carrying me will slow you too much." She gestured to the quickly narrowing stretch of beach before them. "Look!" She struggled to be free. "Put me down, I can manage! You must hurry." She was half out of her mind with concern for his safety. Dearest God! Forbid that he should drown because he had come down from the safety of the cliffs to save *her*!

Off balance from her fighting him, he stopped the steady progress her added weight enabled him to make through the tumultuous waves. He looked down the line of surf. The sea had won. There was too little time left to reach the next path upward.

He looked down into her face, so near his own, and knew that even if he had been born a coward who might desert a woman to save himself, he would not have put her down. He saw with the clarity that only danger brings that life would not be the same if the woman he held in his arms were not part of it.

Whatever power her nearness exerted over him, he felt suddenly complete with her there in his arms. Even the prospect of dying was unimportant next to the fact that he held this woman close.

Standing there with his dark hair dripping sea water down his face, his gaze locked with hers, Moreland defied the power of nature to overcome the strength of his feelings. And while he stood, the tide rolled inexorably to the foot of the cliffs, cutting them off from the path that would have taken them upward and saved them from the sea.

Valerie and Perseus had been running along the cliff tops, keeping pace with the pair who toiled toward safety below them.

"She has fallen!" Perseus cried.

"But he has her!" Valerie shouted back, pushing her wind-tangled hair back so that she could see. "Edward is strong. He can carry her." Valerie clutched at the young butler's sleeve as she leaned dangerously forward for a better look. "Oh! They must hurry!"

Perseus threw a protective arm around Valerie and groaned. "They'll never make it unless she can run, too."

"Oh, look! They have reached the next stretch of beach!"

"Why the devil is he stopping?" Perseus all but screamed.

Suddenly an icy voice came from just behind them. "What the deuce are you doing clutching Lady Valerie in that familiar manner, Wilson?"

A startled Perseus, tried beyond endurance, yelled, "Lytton! Damn and blast you! You are safe!"

"Harry!" Valerie let go of Perseus's sleeve to throw herself against the Lieutenant's chest, sobbing.

Lytton demanded, "Are you all right, dearest?" He bent his head to her wind-blown blond one. His arm gathered her close to him in possessive mastery. He kissed the top of her head, then her forehead, then stood glowering at Perseus as he awaited an explanation.

Perseus, racked by fear for Rosalind, shouted, "Yes, kiss her, you ass! God and everyone else knows you love the chit! But you'd better put your mind to helping think of a way to save her brother, or she'll be in black a year and you'll have to wait to marry her."

Lytton thrust Valerie back away from the cliff as he hurled himself nearer the edge. "Moreland, by God. What is he doing down there? He'll drown!"

"He went after the housekeeper, dearest." Valerie spoke the endearment with wonder. Only the danger that threatened her brother and Mrs. Rose kept stars out of her eyes.

"And the housekeeper is down there because Lady Valerie thought that *you* were in need of rescue." Perseus's anger was evident in his voice even over the wind and surf.

Lytton looked puzzled. "But Ann and I came up the other path. She was afraid we would be caught by the tide if we stayed on the beach longer."

Valerie descended from her rosy cloud with a thud. "Just what were you doing on the beach with Ann?" All the anger, forgotten in the face of danger, surged up again and overwhelmed her.

Lytton saw the signs of an impending fit of temper in his equally beloved Valerie and hastened to speak. "Ann was playing Cupid. She was sternly informing me that I had more gall than anyone had a right to." He drew his darling gently back into the circle of his arm. "She is of the opinion that I am handsome, healthy, and rich enough not to have to worry about losing the roof over my head—though I am at a loss to know why she threw that into my catalog of virtues." He ignored a snort from the butler, who knew all too well why such a comment would be in the forefront of his sister's mind, and went on. "She informed me that I was loved by a beautiful young lady and am the biggest fool God ever made." He stilled his beloved's objection with a quick kiss and went on. "She thinks a little thing like the loss of my arm is a poor excuse for the moping I have been doing."

Valerie rallied at that and added her weight to Andromeda's arguments. "She is perfectly right about that!"

Perseus was at the edge of the cliff gesturing wildly. The lovers knew instant contrition at having forgotten the plight of the two people below them on the rocks.

Lytton quickly kissed Valerie again and stated, "I'll go for help. Ropes and horses and men to drag them up."

Valerie went back and looked down over the edge to where Perseus was staring. The sea was as high as her brother's hips, and she was filled with terror. Her knees gave way with the awful dread that assailed her.

"Dear God! There is no way Harry can be back in time to save them!"

Chapter 19

Rosalind held her breath as, grim-faced, Moreland climbed higher on the headland with her clasped in his arms. The slippery rocks conspired with the sea to defeat him, and her heart turned over with each misstep.

Rosalind looked up at him, silently demanding that he put her down by gently pushing at his chest. "I can walk now," she insisted. He seemed not to hear her.

Suddenly, beyond Moreland, movement on the cliff top caught her eye. "Look! Perseus is trying to tell us something!" she cried over the sound of pounding waves.

Moreland turned to see. The butler was making wide pointing gestures, pointing again and again to the base of the cliff where the headland jutted out from it. "What the devil is he about?" Moreland roared in frustration.

"Of course! The caves!" Rosalind cried. "If we can

get into the caves and climb above the high water mark in time, we will be safe!"

Moreland didn't seem to hear her. She squirmed out of his arms and stood in the circle of them to keep them from being pulled off the rocks by the undertow. "Caves!" She yelled in the direction of his ear, her lips inches from his cheek. "There are caves, hurry!" She tried to push him toward possible safety, tried to make him see.

"Caves? We'll be trapped!"

"No! Come!" She shoved away from him, seized his hand, and began tugging him in the direction Perseus had indicated. The caves! Why hadn't she remembered them? She plowed desperately on through water that was now, even on the higher ground Moreland had won for them, up to her waist. She dragged at the Viscount's hand, willing him to understand they had a chance.

A mighty wave washed over them. Rosalind gasped as she was torn from the rocks and swept out toward the hungry sea. Desperately she held on to Moreland's hand. She felt his arm crack with the strain of holding her against the savage tide, but he held her. She could feel the determination with which he held both the rock he clutched with his left hand and Rosalind's own slender fingers.

Above the roar of the waves, she heard his cursing. He hauled her back to him and held her against his side in a grip that took her breath away.

"Where the hell are these damned caves?" he demanded through clenched teeth.

"There!" Rosalind pointed at a seemingly solid cliff face.

Moreland fought their way toward the spot. As

he clawed his way upward the last few impossible feet, the water sucked at their legs, dragging him back, fighting to overcome them. Rosalind prayed fervently as, with the last of his strength, he seized a long sharp blade of rock for one final, agonizing move shoreward.

"Yes! Yes!" Rosalind cried, tears of relief starting in her eyes. "You have done it! We are safe!"

She pointed, and watched the triumph on Moreland's face as he looked and saw, beyond the rock he had just grabbed, the Stygian darkness that meant a cave.

Even as Rosalind sent a prayer of gratitude skyward, the mightiest wave of them all surged against the cliff and buried them deep in foaming danger.

"Can you see them?" Valerie shook Perseus's arm in a frenzy. "Are they safe? Can you see them?" she shrieked.

Perseus's face was grave, his eyes wild with anxiety as he strained to see through the boiling surf that had just washed over the two below. In the swirling water and flying spray it was impossible to make out whether Rosalind and Moreland had been able to cling to the rock or had been swept away.

He turned to look at Valerie, wondering whether to tell her he didn't know, or to permit her to cherish hope until the tide went out in the morning and they could search the caves. Or find the bodies on the evening tide.

Valerie studied his face, then threw herself against him, her little fists pounding his chest. "Tell me! Tell me the truth! Did you see them taken by the sea? Did you?"

Hooves thundered close by. Lytton arrived at a gallop and yanked the horse to a sliding stop. He flung himself off and rushed to them. Across his body he wore coils of rope. Rope enough to reach down the long face of the cliff and pull Rosalind and Moreland to safety. "Are they still there?" he shouted.

One look at Perseus's face gave him his answer. Staggered, he exclaimed, "Dear God!" Blindly he reached his arm out for Valerie.

Perseus came to them. "There is a chance. They might have escaped by taking refuge in the caves under the headland." He paused to draw a shuddering breath and looked earnestly at Lytton. "But I didn't see whether or not they gained the cave mouth. They were hit by a monstrous wave just as they reached it."

Valerie sobbed softly into Lytton's shirtfront. He stroked her hair in an unconscious effort to comfort her. To Perseus he said, "How will we know? What can we do?"

"There is nothing to do." Perseus voice was husky with emotion. "There is nothing to do but wait for the morning and low tide. If they are safely in the caves, they will emerge when the tide goes out." He left the alternative unspoken.

Lytton faced it unflinchingly. "And if they were swept out into the Channel? Moreland is a strong swimmer. There's a chance for him."

Both Lytton and Perseus knew that attempting to save Rosalind would cut that chance down drastically. All three of them knew Moreland would never abandon the attempt—even if that attempt cost him his life.

Lytton asked after a long moment, "Is there a boat?"

Perseus jumped as if shot. "God! Curse me for a fool. There's my boat. The *Windmaiden*. Hurry."

Men were arriving now carrying more rope. MacFie and Gates led them. Lytton pushed Valerie toward them. "Take care of Lady Valerie!" he shouted as he ran awkwardly after Perseus.

Perseus pounded toward the path Andromeda and Lytton had taken up from the beach what now seemed so long ago. Reaching it, he plunged down it to a small dinghy stored on a rock ledge above the tidemark. He struggled to launch it, glancing back to see if Lytton had come.

Lytton hurled himself down the path and slid on the loose rocks toward where Perseus held the dinghy.

Immediately Perseus pushed off and rowed them out to a trim sloop moored to a floating buoy a hundred yards out.

When they reached the *Windmaiden*, Perseus unceremoniously dragged the one-armed man aboard by his shirtfront.

"Thanks!" Lytton gasped. He was too astonished to feel his customary resentment. After a moment he grinned. Maybe he had been taking himself far too seriously, as the little chambermaid had scolded him. Smiling pensively, the settled himself in the boat and watched the graceful precision with which the butler set sail and got them under way.

Perseus shoved the tiller over hard as the sail caught the wind, sending them back in the direction

of the headland. Lytton moved carefully to the bow
and began to scan the water's surface for any trace
of a swimmer.

A movement off to his right caught his eye, and
he gestured to Perseus at the rudder. Perseus lay the
trim craft over as he answered Lytton's gesture.
There was something in the water just off the port
bow.

"There!" Lytton shouted, pointing to where a
sleek dark head bobbed in the water. Perseus held
course for the spot. Both men held their breath in
painful anticipation. Which of the two who had
struggled so valiantly on the beach was it? Who had
survived that awful wave to be swept here still able
to keep afloat in the surging tide?

As they approached the swimmer, Perseus called
to Lytton, "There's a boat hook . . ."

Lytton waved the hook at him before he could
finish.

Both men strained forward, hope bursting in
them, their gazes riveted to the sleek dark head in
the water. As this distance it could be either one of
them. But there was no sign of a second person.

As they drew near, Perseus nosed the boat into
the wind, losing way, and mentally braced himself.
Would it be Moreland? Or might it be his well-
loved sister-in-law?

"Dear God." Over the roar of the water dashing
against the cliffs and the wind tearing at the luffing
sail, he heard himself fervently pray as he watched
Lytton stretch out along the spray-washed forward
deck and reach out with the boat hook toward the
head in the water.

Chapter 20

Wave-battered and breathless, Rosalind and Moreland squeezed through the narrow aperture. Gasping for air, they stood in water to their chests. Each
pushed sea-drenched hair back out of their eyes to
see that they were at the foot of a tunnel in the rock.

The darkness was unrelieved except for the pale,
eerie glow of fading daylight that ebbed and flowed
with the strong movement of the water. They were
sealed off from their world as effectively as if they
no longer existed in it.

Rosalind groped for Moreland's hand. "Come,
we must go higher." She had to speak loudly to be
heard over the dull booming of the surf that reverberated in the narrow confines of their sanctuary.
"Even here the water will rise." She turned and
struggled to attain the high ledge that was the
beginning of the tunnel.

Moreland put his hands around her waist and
lifted her to it. "Thank you," she managed through

teeth that she held clenched to keep them from
chattering. She grasped his hand again when he
stood beside her on the ledge. Holding up the front
of her sodden skirt with her free hand, she led the
Viscount up a twisting tunnel that became darker
and darker as they moved farther and farther from
the sea-filled mouth of the cave.

Rosalind stumbled only once. Moreland tried to
catch her but missed in the dark, bumping his
elbow sharply against the living rock of the tunnel
wall. He bit back the curse that rose to his lips,
contenting himself with a grunt.

They pressed on, hesitatingly at first, then with
more confidence as the faintest glimmer of light
appeared far ahead. "Where does the light come
from?" Moreland wanted to know.

"The rock is imperfect. It has small fissures that
let in a bit of light." She said quickly, before he
could begin to hope, "Unfortunately, they are too
small to offer a chance of escape. We shall have to
wait for the tide to recede."

As she ended her speech, Rosalind suddenly
realized that she was going to be forced to spend
the night in this cave with a man who was not a
member of her family. She would be hopelessly
compromised. Ruined.

Moreland, unaware of her discomfort, asked,
"How did you know of this place?"

"I grew up here in this area. One of my childhood
friends showed me the cave when I was seven."

"And Wilson knew you would remember it?"

"Oh, several of us played here frequently. I am
just sorry I didn't think of it myself."

Moreland noticed she didn't answer him about

Wilson, but he let it pass without comment. "Didn't your parents object? The tides constitute a very real danger, do they not?"

"My mother died when I was very young," Rosalind answered in a low voice. "My father was frequently away. He was in the army, you will remember." Her voice took on a lighter tone. "And there is very little danger if you come here just before low tide."

"They will be concerned about us at the castle."

"Yes, but Per . . . ah, Wilson will tell them we are safe."

Moreland had no intention of telling her that he wasn't certain those watching from the cliff would know they were safe. That last wave had very nearly thrown them back to the sea, and in the foaming confusion . . . ?

Deliberately he changed the subject. "I think there might be sufficient draft through those fissures to enable us to have a fire, Mrs. Rose—if that was driftwood we stumbled on in the tunnel."

"I can think of nothing I would like more, but how would we light it? We are both most thoroughly soaked."

He chuckled. "Right you are, but I think I can contrive if you would like a fire."

She laughed low in her throat, and Moreland was suddenly deeply aware of her—as aware as he had been that night in the study. He heard her say, "Truly, there is nothing I would like better." He heard a tremor in her voice and realized she must be shivering.

A moment later he heard the sound of her wet

skirts dragging across the cave. "Where are you going?"

"I know my way about, and you do not. There are low spots that you might crack your head on. I'll get the driftwood."

"Guide me. I shall help . . . *Blast it!*"

"Oh, dear. I told you there were low spots." She touched his forehead, her cold fingers searching out the bump. "Oh, dear," she said again. "Does it hurt very badly?"

He stood, half smiling, and enjoyed the play of her soothing fingers on his outraged forehead a moment before he said, "It's nothing, a light bump, merely." He chuckled ruefully. "I should have listened to you."

"I detest people who say I told you so." There was suppressed laughter in her comment.

His laughter boomed in the cavern. "And yet you have just as effectively said it, have you not?"

She laughed with him. "Yes, I suppose I have. Sometimes I am perfectly odious."

Chuckling, he reached out to her. "Here is my hand. Obviously I must be led."

She took his hand in as brisk and impersonal manner as she could manage, confused by the feelings that swept through her as his strong fingers closed over her own.

They found the wood largely by feeling for it. They searched all the way down to where the dull-booming surf gurgled and sucked hungrily at the lowest point of the tunnel. The search brought them a few more bumps from the irregular rock walls. Finally they had gathered as much as Rosalind could pile on the willing arms of the Viscount.

"I think I can see you well enough to follow you back toward the light." His deep voice seemed to fill the passage.

Moreland was beginning to feel the chill of the cave. As he did, he worried about her. What must she be feeling in her lighter garments?

By the time they had piled the wood neatly in the cave, Rosalind, without even that small exertion to warm her, was shivering so badly she could no longer hide it from her companion.

She heard Moreland reach into his clothing. It sounded to her as if he were handling a delicate metal. An instant later she saw his handsome profile in a tiny spark of light.

"Fire! Oh, what a delightful surprise! I think I must not have believed you could do it!" Eagerly she knelt beside him on the rough rock floor.

The Viscount grinned up at her. "Never doubt that I can do whatever I say I can do."

"I shan't ever again if you will only make it warm for just a moment," she promised as she hugged arms around herself in a futile effort to stop shivering.

He knew she was smiling at him. He knew, too, that she was desperately cold. He could feel her body shaking in the darkness beside his own. Alarm rose in him. He'd not forgotten that she'd left a sickbed to go to the rescue of his sister and Lytton.

Concern for her made his hand tremble as he struck a spark to the fuzzy silvers of driftwood he had shaved for tinder. What if the draft in the cave was insufficient to draw the smoke out through the fissures and he had to extinguish even the small blaze he planned to test it? How would he keep her warm? How could he ensure that she would not develop a serious illness from being wet when she was already suffering from a cold?

How would he keep her warm . . . and keep his honor?

Chapter 21

Lytton and Valerie stood silently at the window overlooking the headland where Moreland and the housekeeper had disappeared in a boil of foaming surf.

"Do you think there is a chance, Harry?" She whispered her next words. "Please tell me there is a chance."

Lytton, stirred to his depths by her mournful tone, slipped his arm around her waist. "There is a very good chance, dearest. Edward has been in tight spots before, you know."

Valerie sighed and valiantly changed the subject. "It must have been awful for you to reach for that swimmer you thought was one of them and find it was only a seal."

Lytton fought down the feeling of desolation that recurred as he remembered that moment. "Yes," he replied simply. Dejection tore at him. Edward Forsythe was the best friend a man could wish for.

What if he had been . . . Valerie felt him tense and stroked his hand. He shook himself mentally and set about cheering Valerie. "Of course, I soon realized that it means they are probably safe."

"Oh?" Valerie turned in his embrace to look up at him eagerly, her eyes shining with hope. "Why do you say so?"

"Because Edward would never have let go of a drowning woman to save himself, and she could not have kept afloat very long in her water-logged skirts. Not unaided."

"Of course, you are right." Valerie looked at him adoringly. "Oh, how terribly glad I am that you are here with me, Harry."

With one accord they resumed their vigil.

In the kitchen, Andromeda, eyes flashing with impatience, demanded of Perseus, "Did you actually see them enter the cave?"

"No, Andy, but I believe they made it inside."

Cassiopeia put a gentle hand on his sleeve. "You do? Really?" Cassie needed to be strongly reassured that their dear sister-in-law was safe—that both were safe. She'd not been able to bear the thought of death since the loss of her brother Hermes.

Castor and Pollux stood anxiously watching the others. Finally they could contain themselves no longer. Eyes wide with avid interest they speculated. "If they didn't get into the cave . . ." Castor began.

". . . were they drowned?" Pollux finished.

The twins looked from Perseus to Andromeda. "If they drowned . . ." Castor said.

". . . then will we find them all bloated and fish chewed on the evening tide?"

Pollux's words had an explosively devastating effect on the spirits of those around them. Cassiopeia burst into tears. Cook threw down her bowl of pea pods to rush from her chair by the fire and charge across the room. She snatched Cassie into comforting arms and began patting the sobbing girl. "Now, now. There now," she murmured soothingly. "They'll be fine, just you wait and see." Over Cassie's shoulder she frowned at the thoughtless boys.

"You two little beasts be still or get out!" Perseus glowered at the Gemini. "I won't have you upsetting the ladies with your careless comments, you little ghouls."

Startled, the Gemini scuttled for safety out the back door. They'd go to the stables. They'd be safe there. Certainly MacFie would be able to tell them what chance their favorite aunt had. And a lot less emotionally, too.

In the cave in the headland, Rosalind watched as Moreland nursed the feeble glow he had ignited to a bright little flame. Carefully feeding twigs into the minuscule conflagration, he soon had a small campfire built under one of the fissures in the rock. Sitting back on his heels, he said with relief, "I think the smoke is going out of the cave." He glanced at her in the firelight. He was filled with concern, seeing the shivering she could not suppress. His voice tensed. "I shall build the fire larger very slowly. Stop me if the first bit of smoke lingers."

"Indeed I shall, for I've no wish to choke in it, I

assure you." There was humor in her comment in spite of the cold and its effect on her.

Moreland heard the chuckle in her voice and wondered if it meant she were as brave as he thought her, or if her laughter signaled some sort of nervous crisis. He'd little experience with women in difficult situations and could only rely on the stories other men had told him. Doing so made him uncomfortable.

Rosalind sensed his discomfort. "I am only cold and wet." She managed a tight little smile. "Neither are things I have never before experienced, I assure you. Your fire will take care of both in time." She laughed at his expression. "I am not a grenade about to explode in your face, Your Lordship. Please do not look so dismayed."

"A grenade." He settled back on his heels and watched her face in the firelight. "That's an interesting comment. Not many women of my acquaintance have a working knowledge of grenades."

Rosalind's smile faded. "You know I am a soldier's daughter, Your Lordship." Sadness marred her brow, and she added so softly that he could not hear, "And a soldier's widow." A moment passed as she looked down at the flames.

And in that moment, Moreland was shaken to his very core. That face! *Hers* was the face that had haunted his dreams since that long-ago mission into Spain. Dear God! Was it any wonder her presence had caused a stir in him? She—she, his very housekeeper—was the woman against whose memory he had measured every woman he'd met since that magic moment he had first seen her!

He was dumbfounded. If she'd made a comment

to which he needed to reply, it would have been beyond him to have done so. He felt exuberant as a boy, wanting to dance her around the fire and shout at her the joy he felt at having rediscovered her. He felt as burdened as an old man—burdened by family loyalties and social traditions that would keep them apart as surely as if they had never again met in this present world.

His emotions buffeting him with greater strength than had the waves from the Channel, Moreland sat, statue-still, and drank in the serene beauty of *her* face. When finally he trusted himself to speak he asked mundanely, in as normal a voice as he could muster, "Are you warmer?"

She smiled then, with a courage that broke his heart. "Much better," she said, hugging her knees to her chest as she sat as close to the fire as she dared.

Mentally he assessed the remaining wood, then built the fire a little higher.

"Ummmm, that is lovely." Rosalind smiled her thanks. Valiantly she tried to control her shivering.

"You are so cold, and I haven't a dry coat to offer you."

Rosalind looked at him, her eyes curious, wondering about the tension she sensed in him. Finally she said in her low voice, "We are equally damp. But the fire will dry us." She went on, trying to put him at ease. "How did you manage to strike a spark to the tinder when you are soaking wet?

He reached into a pocket and drew out the tiny silver tinderbox he carried. "Here is my secret," he said, smiling. "I had this made by a jeweler years ago to take with me into the army." He handed her the beautifully chased little container.

Rosalind suppressed a gasp as she took it from the palm of his extended hand. She'd felt as if a spark had been struck between his hand and her own.

Moreland watched, shrugging with difficulty out of his coat, as she turned the box in her slender fingers. "The jeweler was clever, was he not? See how closely he has fitted the joints to make it proof against the entry of water."

While she examined the tinderbox, he took two heavy pieces of driftwood and braced them to hold his coat up near the fire. Later, *if* it dried, he would use it to help keep her warm.

"Indeed," Rosalind marveled, "the closure is so tight that it is easy to see why the seawater did not find its way in. How very ingenious." She turned admiring eyes to him.

"Thank you." He tucked the proffered box back into its pocket. "Soldiers are often ingenious when it comes to ways of assuring themselves a little comfort."

She laughed as she remembered. "Yes, they certainly are."

Moreland seized this opening to ask the question that sought to burst his heart. "You followed the drum?" He held his breath waiting for her reply. Had she gone with the army as a camp follower? He felt pain lash him at the very thought. Yet he himself had seen her at that campfire with no gold band on her hand to signify marriage. Agony assailed him as he waited an eternity for her reply.

"Yes. My husband was in the cavalry. . . ."

Moreland's head spun and his heart sang. She could have told him her husband had been in the damned *French* cavalry and he would have rejoiced. She had been a wife! She was honorable, his heart was not betrayed! He could breathe again.

With the first breath he said, "I apologize if I have caused you pain in bringing back the memory."

For some reason she was unable to fathom, she found herself saying, "It has been almost two years. And ours was the marriage of good friends rather than a grand passion." She met his eyes, and her next words seemed to come of their own accord. "Hermes sensed that he would not survive the war, and I fled with him from an unwanted marriage to a man many years my senior." Color suffused her face, rosy in the firelight. What had possessed her to speak so intimately to a man she hardly knew?

Moreland, his heart striving to soar from his very frame, contrived to look busy tending the fire. In a voice he strove to keep calm, he asked, "I suggest you turn and toast your back for a while."

"Yes, thank you," Rosalind said uncertainly as she turned.

He sensed she was uncomfortable because of what she had told him. He was too overjoyed by her words to trust himself to attempt to put her at ease, however.

After all, he could hardly tell her that *he* was, and somehow fully intended to be, the grand passion of her life.

Chapter 22

Rosalind shivered and hugged her knees tighter in a vain effort to get warm. Even with Moreland's fire, the temperature in the cave seemed to drop with the deepening of night.

Moreland asked, "Are you cold?"

"I am f-fine," she lied between chattering teeth.

"The devil you are!" He growled in frustration, angry to see her trapped in a situation that forced her gallant lie. Without thought he reached for her and hauled her over against him, enfolding her in his arms.

Shocked, Rosalind was absolutely still, her mind whirling, overset by her body's tingling reaction. How on earth could she stay locked in his embrace, however well meaning? The impropriety of her position made her head spin. She was very much in a quandary.

Moreland's thought, too, troubled him. How the blazes could he justify spending the night with a decent woman to whom he was not married clasped in his arms? Damn society's censure! He would be even less able to justify to himself letting his housekeeper die of exposure while he played the prude!

Rosalind made as if to move away from him, and his arms tightened. He held her firmly against the hard muscles of his chest. "This is warmer. For both of us," he said gruffly.

She was still, realizing he intended to hold her. She consoled her conscience by remembering that soldiers often huddled together to stay warm through a cold night—trying to convince herself that she might stay here in his arms where the warmth from his body was beginning to seep into her own half-frozen one.

Moreland sensed her surrender, then felt her take a breath as if to speak. Wanting nothing more to make his position difficult, he placed a hand along the side of her face and pressed her cheek firmly against his chest. "Go to sleep," he ordered roughly.

"Halloo! Are you safe? Are you here?" Perseus's voice rang through the tunnel and reverberated around the cave above.

Rosalind was startled from sleep. Her eyes flew open to see those of the Viscount regarding her lazily—from a completely inadequate distance!

To her acute embarrassment, she discovered that she had turned to face him in the night. She had put her arms around his neck, and until Perseus's cry had awakened her, she'd had her cheek pressed against the strong column of his throat. Never had she been so embarrassed! What must he be thinking? She'd never slept so . . . so . . . She had never slept *so*! Even with Hermes! Turning away to hide her blushes, she rose so suddenly she tripped over her skirts.

Moreland rose, too, and taking his coat from the driftwood on which it had been drying all night, placed it about her shoulders. Then he stretched and shrugged himself fully awake. In spite of the rocky floor that had served them as bed, he had never slept better.

Perseus erupted into the dim cave, the Gemini in joyous pursuit.

While the Winstons rushed Rosalind down to the kitchen for a comfortable warming by the big kitchen fireplace, Valerie and Lytton counseled Moreland to take full advantage of the bath they'd had prepared for him the moment the tide turned.

Moreland, one arm encircling Valerie and the other thrown across the shoulders of his friend, watched the chattering group of servants bear Rosalind away, a pensive look on his face. Not one voice was of the serving class—and he was not surprised. His heart lifted when, at the last moment, *she* turned her face back for a glimpse of him.

"Harry. I'll soak longer if you will bear me company."

"I should be glad to." He shot a meaningful glance at Valerie. "There is something I wish to discuss with you."

Settled luxuriously in his steaming tub, Moreland regarded his friend. He had a good idea what it was Lytton wished to discuss.

"Edward, old chap."

Moreland waited.

"Uh, I say, Edward . . ." Lytton's anguished eyes met his.

Moreland put him out of his misery. "You have my blessings."

Harry Lytton flew from his chair, unable to still his joy. "Thank you, Edward," he managed after two rapid circles of the tub, "I swear you'll never regret it!"

Moreland looked at him with lifted brows. "My only hope is that you do not," he said dryly.

"She's an angel. Who would have thought I'd be smitten by the little girl who tagged after us? Why, I've loved her since she was a child. No woman could interest me once she had captured my heart! Her letters were all that kept me going while . . ."

So this was love. Moreland stopped listening to his friend's transports and turned his thoughts inward. Love began when one least expected it and continued with no regard for reason. Love gave a man such exuberance of spirit, did it? He consulted his own heart. Yes, he loved her. He could feel his love like a hawk fighting its tether, fighting to soar. He loved her. Impossible as that love was, he loved . . . *Dammit! What was her name?*

Chapter 23

More than the fate of Valerie and Lytton was decided while Moreland soaked warmth back into his body. When Lytton came back to earth, he had the presence of mind to inform his future brother-in-law that Attleborough had expressed a wish to see him.

Moreland chuckled. Sir Richard had undoubtedly issued an order for him to present himself at the War Office, and it was Lytton's euphoric state of mind that had softened that order to a request.

"Was there anything special Sir Richard wanted?" he asked gently.

"Ummm?" Lytton was having difficulty keeping his mind on apprehending spies. "Oh. Yes, he said he'd need you two days, beginning Wednesday. Wants the meeting to look like a casual one, so he asks that you show up at Almack's. He'll seem to bump into you there."

"Almack's! God. Knee britches."

Lytton grinned. "Shall I alert Gates? Sir Richard wants him to drive your town coach to Almack's."

"Interesting." Moreland flipped a hand in the direction of the towel that warmed near the fireplace. Lytton tossed it to him and went in search of Gates.

"I'm to accompany you. Good." Gates's low voice rumbled close to Moreland's ear as the valet smoothed the shoulders of his coat.

For a breath Moreland hesitated. "Yes," he said finally. He smiled at the effort it cost him not to insist that Gates remain at the castle, the devil with orders. Things must be coming to a head in the investigation, however, and it was impossible to leave Gates here to see to the safety and welfare of . . . his love. *Blast it! He still didn't know her name!*

With the necessity to be in London to meet his superior at the ball at Almack's pressing him, he sent for Wilson.

"Wilson, I shall be absent for three days. Look to Mrs. Rose's health. Remember she left her sickbed to go down on the beach. Call the physician instantly if she is no more than a trifle indisposed. Please watch her carefully—" He cut off his sentence sharply, almost having added "for me." He felt himself color under Wilson's speculative gaze. "And convey to her my gratitude for having saved my life."

"Saved your life!" Perseus couldn't contain himself. "If you hadn't gone down there to save hers, she'd have drowned!"

"You will please convey my message, nevertheless. It was her knowledge of the cave that saved us."

Perseus opened his mouth to proclaim that it was his own signal about the cave and the Viscount's strength that had saved the day. One look at the Viscount, who watched him closely, his expression intent, convinced him to hold his peace. "Very well, Your Lordship, it shall be just as you say."

"Thank you."

The horses were brought round. By riding, they would make better time to the capital—and better time returning.

At Almack's, Attleborough walked casually past Moreland. He nodded in a offhandedly friendly fashion as he went, halted two strides beyond the Viscount, then turned back as if to chat.

Moreland, resplendent in white satin small clothes and a black coat, brought his seemingly absorbed attention away from a group of debutantes with feigned reluctance and bowed politely.

Sir Richard said in a light conversational voice, "I have your reports on my desk. They, when combined with the reports from Talbot, further down the coast, give us a pretty clear idea of how many are involved.

"It looks like we can eliminate Mr. Cox. That gentleman seems to live so much under the cat's foot he is given no latitude to spy." He nodded affably to a couple who walked past to join the next set on the dance floor.

Moreland smiled and bowed briefly to them. About Cox, he silently agreed.

Smiling broadly as if talking inconsequentialities, Attleborough said, "That leaves Alton and Radley. And since we are certain there are at least two men involved, I think you will want to consider both highly suspect."

"Radley is a likeable chap. Pity."

"Alton?" Attleborough asked.

"Nice enough, I suppose. Rather free with his opinions."

"Well, keep on it. Next week we spring the trap. I have complete cooperation from the navy. All shipping will be blockaded on Wednesday, when we leak the information, and until we catch the traitors. As you can imagine, there is going to be an outcry from the shipping merchants, so pray it moves swiftly." He took a large white linen handkerchief to his face and the back of his neck and complained in a louder voice as two gentlemen passed close by, "Why the deuce do they keep ballrooms the temperature of hothouses, Moreland?"

The Viscount murmured something inane about the flowers of young womanhood, and the two men were gone.

Attleborough finished their business. "Gates has the necessary warrants at your coach by now. Good hunting, lad." He clapped a hand to Moreland's shoulder in parting. "Now go and do the pretty with the lovelies. God knows the mammas are in alt to see you here. Make old Silence and the rest of the Patronesses think you've come to their marriage mart to choose Viscountess Moreland, and nobody will remember that you stood in conversation with this old man for ten minutes." With a twinkle in his eye, he walked away.

The hapless Moreland, with every appearance of a man impatient after a dull conversation, went with pretended enthusiasm to do as he'd been ordered.

Moreland and Gates left the hustle and bustle of London without regret. The Viscount left behind a score of frustrated mothers and disappointed debutantes. He'd spent the whole time he'd danced with the latter comparing the young lovelies in their fabulous gowns to one he had left at Castle Winston in a simple gray dress. Now that he had more than a well-remembered face to compare them with, none of the girls so breathlessly eager to captivate the handsome, rich Lord Moreland had the slightest chance of engaging his interest.

The Viscount and his valet left London before dawn. They breathed the clean sea air on the last leg of their journey with as much enthusiasm as did their weary horses.

Moreland heard the gatekeeper toll the bell that signaled visitors to Castle Winston as they cantered through the tall iron gates.

Minutes later, when he reached the castle, he found waiting for him on the wide steps with his butler not only Lytton and Valerie, but also his housekeeper—warned by the bell of his approach.

As he dismounted and gave his reins to the waiting groom, he fought to keep his eyes properly on his sister and his future brother-in-law. All the time he was greeting them, *her* presence pulled at him like a magnet.

Passing her on his way into the house, their glances caught. Was he mistaken? Was she as glad to see him? "I would like to see you in the study, Mrs. Rose. In an hour, when I have changed out of my dirt, please."

"Certainly, Your Lordship."

He found her voice musical. After the simpering giggles of the debutantes of the *ton*, it was angelsong. He carried it carefully in his memory as he went to bathe and change.

Rosalind, her duties done, decided to pass the hour she must wait to see Moreland again in walking on the cliffs. She left the house and turned unconsciously in the direction of her former home. When she realized it, she'd almost turned back, remembering the narrow escape she'd had when she'd almost met her father the day she went riding.

She chided herself for her excuse of caution. She was not mounted on a fleet Thoroughbred now. She smiled to herself. She would hardly attain so far as her father's boundary on shanks' mare.

The brisk wind from the Channel tugged at her light cloak, and she turned her face into it, breathing deeply the tang of the salt air, holding firmly to her hood, remembering. She'd intended to remember the days of her childhood, but the memory of her night in the cave with Moreland intervened.

Moreland. Her heart lightened whenever she thought of him. Her mind filled with memories of his strength and the gallantry with which he had refused to leave her to save himself. Hard on the heels of that memory came that of the length of his firm body holding her, sharing his warmth. And offering her not the slightest offense. Truly he was a very great gentleman.

"Careful, my girl," she told herself aloud. "You are in very grave danger of falling in love with the Viscount." Even as she voiced the words, she knew she lied. She was already hopelessly in love with the quiet, grave-eyed man who was presently master of Castle Winston.

She heaved a great sigh. "Oh!" Her eyes flew open and her sigh turned into a startled gasp as she rounded a bend in the path and came face to face with a threat from her past! Bitwell!

She ducked her head hastily, hoping to hide her identity in the shadow of her hood. Too late! She saw the flash of recognition and the flare of glaring hatred in his eyes.

With an inarticulate roar, he reached out for her, but she had already turned to flee, and all he caught was the back of her cloak. As his fist closed on the fabric of her cape, his cruel laugh of triumph rang out.

Gulls, settling on the cliff rocks for the night, rose in a startled cloud. Shrieking their protest, they wheeled into the darkening sky. Rosalind clawed frantically at the loose knot at her throat and left her cape in her captor's hands as she ran back the way she had come. Fear threatened to steal her strength. She was terrified to see, face to face, the nature she had hitherto only sensed in her father's friend.

As she fled with all her might for the safety of the castle, she hard a sound that chilled her blood and lent wings to her feet. Casting a quick glance back over her shoulder, she saw the well-respected General Bitwell snarlingly rip her cloak in two with superhuman strength. In the fading light she saw his head thrown back as he howled like a wild animal deprived of its prey.

In the well-appointed study Moreland paced like a caged beast, his thoughts driving him like a trainer's whip. What to say? How could he express what he wanted her to know without sounding like a fool? Worse yet, suppose he should fail to turn her to his purpose?

He ran a hand distractedly through his hair and looked toward the door for the tenth time in as many minutes. And she was there.

Rosalind entered the room trying to smile. "Your Lordship." Her voice trembled.

Moreland was instantly at her side. "What is it? What has frightened you?" Seeing her gray eyes big with pain and fright, he snatched her into his arms. "What has frightened you, my dear brave love?"

Rosalind, her emotions raw after her encounter with the man she had fled long years before and just now, her nerves tried after her narrow escape from the sea and her body exhausted by her terrifying run over the cliffs, could be brave no longer. She buried her face in the Viscount's perfect cravat and sobbed as if her heart would break.

Moreland, astonished but overjoyed to feel her arms convulsively clasping him, was momentarily powerless to do more than hold her and let the sensations triggered by her nearness wash over him. Without speaking, his lips against her hair, he held her as the storm in her broke around them.

When her sobs began to subside, he led her to the

small settee beside the fireplace and sat with her on it. With a gentle touch, he lifted her face to his. The firelight played across her tear-marked face, and he wondered if he would ever see firelight without thinking of her.

Even after a flood of weeping she was the loveliest of creatures. "What is it?" he asked softly. "You must tell me what could frighten my brave girl so."

Rosalind heard the possessive note in his voice and could not help the way her heart rejoiced. "It was nothing—a nightmare from the past. I am fine, I assure you. Forgive me for acting like a watering pot."

He held her away from him with hands hard with anger. "Tell me," he demanded, his eyes stormy.

Rosalind rose and he released her. She turned her back to him—the gesture symbolic of her necessity to shut him out of her affairs, out of her life. His desperate concern was misplaced when it was directed to a servant. She could never be more to him under the circumstances.

"Do you refuse to tell me?" His voice was a bitter balance between ice and pain.

Rosalind was not proof against his appeal. "It was a . . . suitor from my past. From before my marriage. He was not . . . he was not happy to lose me to my husband."

"Has he offered you insult?" She felt, behind her, Moreland seem to increase in stature with his demand.

"No." That was truth. Bitwell had, if his eyes had spoken his feelings, offered her not insult but murder. "No," she said softly, trembling to remember the man's insane rage. "He was merely . . . unpleasant." That was certainly true. She struggled to suppress the shudder she felt at the memory of General Bitwell rending the sturdy fabric of her cloak.

With shaking hands she wiped the traces of tears from her face and turned to face Moreland. She made a helpless little gesture with her hands. "I am merely overwrought. The ordeal of the sea—I am just weary." She smiled at him tremulously. "Women can be very silly when they are tired, Your Lordship."

Moreland was overwhelmed by a feeling of helplessness. The chasm society's conventions had placed between them had never yawned wider. "Have you supped, Mrs. Rose?"

"Yes, Your Lordship." She was puzzled by his question.

"I wish you will leave off addressing me as my Lordship when we are alone, Mrs. Rose."

His request threw her into confusion. She was having trouble enough not addressing him as an equal.

"My valet has managed to oblige me in this." When she did not respond, he said briskly, "Very well. If you have had your supper, I shall take the liberty of ordering you to your bed."

She looked at him in astonishment.

"You are quite right. You are weary. I would have you rest."

Quick tears filled Rosalind's eyes. She turned and left the room.

He heard her faint "thank you" from the hall. His

arms felt strangely empty. He could not, however, have insisted she remain in her present state.

A woman should be well rested when a man informs her he is going to marry her.

Chapter 24

The next morning the sun sparkled and glittered across the waves of the Channel with a special brilliance. The gulls mewing in the sky were whiter and more graceful than Moreland had ever seen them. Their raucous cry even sounded musical. He leaned on the chest-high stone wall and grinned like a boy. He was waiting for *her* to answer his summons.

Cassiopeia saw her own shocked face in the mirror over Valerie's head. Her blood ran cold. She could hardly keep her hand rhythmically stroking the brush through Valerie's hair.

". . . So I am certain we will be going back to London any day now, for I saw the paper authorizing the arrest in Edward's desk drawer." Valerie glanced at Cassie in the mirror. "Don't look so shocked. Edward will be discreet. The neighborhood will not be disturbed at all, you'll see."

Cassie stood as if she had been turned to stone. What did she care for the neighbors' thoughts? Or indeed anything else when this horrible thing was going to happen?

Valerie, unaware of the tumult of emotions assaulting Cassie, got up and gave her a quick hug. "But I shall truly miss you when we are gone home!" She ran from the room without a backward glance, eager to find Lytton.

Cassie stood where she had left her like a statue, tears welling. Lord Moreland—a man they had begun to think of as a friend—was about to arrest her beloved brother for smuggling!

Rosalind paused before her mirror before rushing out of her room to answer Moreland's summons. She laughed to see the bright-eyed eagerness of the girl reflected back at her. "You are riding for a fall, milady. The Viscount cannot possibly return your feelings!" she chided herself. Her heart was light, nonetheless, and her feet seemed to fly as they carried her to him.

Humming under her breath, she reached the landing and was nearly knocked down by Cassie, who stumbled heedlessly down the stairs, blinded by tears.

Grabbing the girl to steady her, Rosalind demanded, "What is it? What has upset you, Cassie?" Alarmed, she gave her sister-in-law a little shake. "Dearest, tell me what is wrong!"

Cassie blinked away tears and dragged Rosalind back into her room, closing the door firmly behind them. "Oh, Rosalind. The most dreadful thing! Perseus tried to sell *Windmaiden*, his boat, when we learned we were all but destitute, but we wouldn't let him—just as no one would sell my mare, Queen of Hearts, or Hermes's Thunderer. So, to justify keeping her, he . . . he . . . you know." Her tears started afresh.

"Yes," Rosalind said, impatient to get to the bottom of what had caused her sister-in-law to be this overset. With an effort she made her voice a whisper: "He used her to make a smuggling run to help raise money instead."

"Yes!" Cassie gulped and wiped at her tears with shaking fingers. "And now Moreland is going to arrest him for it."

Rosalind's hand stopped dead in the act of handing Cassie a handkerchief. "No!" Her heart, too, stopped for a moment with the agony of it. He couldn't. Moreland couldn't have come here to spy out and arrest Perseus. She couldn't bear to think that.

"Yes, he is." Cassie mopped fresh tears and shook her head in the affirmative. "Valerie told me she saw the papers authorizing him to do so. She must have played Peter Pry. She said she saw them in his desk drawer. She is so happy to have found that Lytton loves her, she is no longer careful of what she says. Otherwise, I am sure we would never have known."

Rosalind simply stared at her. She felt as fragile as glass, afraid to move for fear she would shatter.

"Oh, Rosalind, what shall we do?"

"I don't know."

"Isn't there something we can do?"

"Try not to worry, Cassie. I am on my way to talk to the Viscount. I'll see if there is anything that can be done." She spoke her assuring words woodenly, out of habit. Her thoughts were in chaos, and truly she had no idea how anything could be made right.

She left Cassie sniffling on the landing and went to meet Moreland with a slow and measured tread. She no longer flew with a light in her heart but moved like a lady on her way to the executioner's block.

The gulls screeched quarrelsomely overhead as she crossed the terrace to Moreland. Was what Cassie said true? She saw the air of suppressed triumph on his face. Was it because he had caught his prey? Was he indeed alight with the exultation of the hunt? The very thought that he could be so glad to have caught such a small offender as Perseus broke her heart. How could she have so misread this man? What was there to glow about in apprehending a mere boy who had made one trip to France to smuggle wines? And that to help his family.

What kind of a monster was Moreland? Her mind filled with anger as her heart died within her. Steeling herself, she said, "You sent for me, Your Lordship?"

Moreland frowned, but even his frown failed to dim the eagerness in his face. "I have asked you to dispense with that form of address when we are alone, my dear," he reminded her.

"How can I do so, under the circumstances?"

Moreland laughed and took her hands. He was so wrapped up in the joy of his decision to have her to wife no matter the cost that he didn't notice the edge in her voice. "My business here is almost at an end, my dear." He kissed her hand, looking at her over it with a strange intensity.

Rosalind snatched her hand away. "So I have been told, Your Lordship." Her voice was cold.

His regard changed subtly. He seemed puzzled, both by her change in attitude toward him and by her knowledge of his activities. Oh, perfidious man that he had come here and been so kind, and all to trap Perseus! She could scarce believe it.

Moreland looked at her earnestly. "What is it, my dear? What is it that has upset you?"

They were the very words she had just said to Cassie! How dare he? In a voice she could barely control she demanded, "How can you ask what has upset me?" She felt rage building. "How dare you come here to hunt down and arrest someone so dear to me and then ask what has upset me?" Heated tears spilled down her cheeks, and her voice shook with the intensity of the emotions tearing at her.

Moreland was stunned. Radley dear to her? It was like a knife in his heart. Radley, a traitor of the first magnitude, held dear by this woman whose husband had given his life opposing the master Radley served? How could this be? He stared at Rosalind incredulously. For his life he could not form a comment to answer her.

Rosalind, however, was suffering no such restraint. "I could not believe it. But now you stand there without making the slightest denial, and I know. You came to Castle Winston only to apprehend him. You let us all like you and find you noble and good. . . . You let us all think you were so kind. . . . You even let me—"

She halted on the brink of that indiscretion. Never would she let him know she loved him. She would find a way to tear the roots of that love from her aching heart if it was the last thing she ever did.

Never would she permit herself to love the man who intended to rend asunder the only family she had known since that heart-crushing day her father had disowned her. "How could you?" she hissed at him vehemently.

Fury exploded in Moreland. "How could I what?" He seized her fragile wrist in a crushing hold. "How could I discover and bring to justice a man who has aided and abetted the enemies of my country?" He changed his grip, both hands grasping her shoulders, and shouted at her, "By all that is holy, *madame*, how in the name of hell can you chastise me for it?"

She struggled vainly to be free of his grasp, loathing his very touch. How could she have thought for a minute that she might have spoken rationally to him and saved Perseus. The man was like a bloodhound on the scent. He cared not a whit for the damage he might do her family. For the terrible damage he was doing her heart. Loathsome, despicable man! She moaned aloud with the pain of it.

Moreland saw the suffering in her eyes, and it further enraged him. How could she love the traitor! He had dared to think, only a moment ago, that she loved *him*. Him! Moreland! He had called her here to tell her he intended to make her his wife even if it meant wounding his family—giving up his title! How could she so betray him?

He shook her then, shook her so thoroughly that

her hair came loose and tumbled down her back. He was seized with the mad desire savagely to bury his fingers in it.

"Let me go!" she demanded, her face pale.

Angered by the hand she placed against his chest to hold him off, he surrendered to the urge and buried his hands in her long, shining hair.

Love a traitor, would she! He yanked her to him, crushing her hand and her breasts against the hard wall of his chest. Spurn *his* love for that of a filthy . . . His mouth ground down on hers punishingly.

He heard her small whimper, but he didn't care. If he could never have her, at least he would have this moment. He kissed her again, mercilessly.

Rosalind felt the strength leave her body, drawn out of her by the passion with which he kissed her. She willed her senses to resist him, but to no avail. She loved him, God forgive her, she loved this man who was about to destroy her family!

Even as she yielded to his plundering mouth, she vowed she would never forgive him, that there could never be anything between them.

His kiss gentled, and became tender. It was more than she could bear. Slow tears burned down her cheeks, and she lay limp in his arms. Through senses he had set awry she heard him ask in a voice that broke, "How could you love him, my dear brave girl? How could someone so true and wonderful love a man like Radley?"

Shock hit her like an icy wave. Radley? Radley! Who in the world was Radley? Her thoughts tumbling wildly, she looked up at him, her tears ceasing and a look of utter bewilderment on her face.

"Who," she asked tremulously, as the vague memory of a name on a list stirred in the back of her mind, "is Radley?"

The French doors from the library slammed open, and Lytton erupted onto the terrace. "The game's afoot! Hurry, Moreland! He's taken the bait and is even now frantically looking for a boat to take him to France."

Moreland looked down at Rosalind. His mind seemed to be ripping in half. Even as he transferred part of his attention to his friend and to the urgent matter at hand, he realized that he must resolve this thing with the woman he loved. And there was no time. Blast it, he had no time!

Lytton grasped his arm and shook it, bringing him back to earth with a thud.

"Edward! Come! For God's sake, we must go!"

With a tremendous effort of will, Moreland released Rosalind. As he hurried away to his duty, still half angry, he called an order back to her. "Prepare to be wed on my return, Madame Housekeeper. You are *mine*, dammit, and I intend to have you!"

With that he went tearing off after Lytton, leaving Rosalind leaning weakly against the stone wall, staring openmouthed after him.

Chapter 25

Rosalind walked back into the castle in a daze. She loved him, and he loved her. She kept reliving the magic of those moments in his arms when her senses swam under the influence of his masterful kisses. Time enough when he returned to think of all the reasons there could never be anything between them.

There was no way she could marry him. To marry him as his social equal, she would have to tell him who she was. And there was no way she could identify herself without shaming her family—particularly her fiercely proud father—by exposing the scandal of their estrangement. And it was beyond thinking of that she would permit Moreland to place himself outside the pale by marrying a servant. The situation was hopeless.

Just now, though, she wanted to fix irrevocably in her mind the memory of the strength of his embrace and the passion of his kisses.

* * *

The hours dragged by and Cook became frantic to know when to have dinner. Perseus haunted the great hall to be there to open the door when Moreland and Lytton arrived. Valerie haunted Perseus, inquiring every five minutes if there was any sign of them.

On top of it all, Rosalind had a moment of extreme concern for Moreland's safety at the point in the afternoon when she descended from her rosy cloud and realized Moreland might be in danger. She had difficulty being cheerful from then on.

When the drumming of the door knocker shattered the peace of the great hall, half the household rushed to answer it. Perseus dragged open the huge oak door to reveal a tall, elegantly garbed gentleman with blood running down the side of his face.

"Father!" Rosalind ran forward to receive the sagging form of her parent into her arms.

"Let me help you, sir!" Perseus cried as he leapt to the Earl of Summerfield's other side and threw an arm around him. Together he and Rosalind half carried the man to the comfort of a chair.

"Oh, Father, what happened?" Rosalind cried as she knelt beside him. "Are you all right?"

"Righter than I deserve to be, girl." He gazed hungrily down into her face. "Can you ever forgive me?"

Rosalind didn't hesitate. "Right now and with all my heart, Father." Her face was aglow.

The Earl peered up at Perseus. "Your brother married her and kept her safe from Bitwell when I would have forced her to marry him. I owe you all a debt of gratitude for that."

Perseus placed a consoling hand on the older man's shoulder.

"I mean it, lad. I've been a poor neighbor, but I'll make it up to you. I'll fix the mess your father made of the estate. My word on it." When it looked as if Perseus would speak in defense of his sire, he held up a hand. "Your father was a fool and gambled his money away. But he wasn't the only old fool on this coast." The Earl of Summerfield sighed heavily. "There are other—worse—ways to be a fool." His voice was bitter.

He turned back to his daughter. "Rosalind, dearest child. Bitwell always knew where you were—always told me you scorned me and were happier with me out of your life. Even when I could have wept to think of you employed by people not good enough to sit at the same table with you, he told me . . . Never mind. Suffice it to say he poisoned my mind every time I wanted to go bring you home. I was seven times a fool to believe him. The man is a traitor!"

Several of the assembled group gasped at his announcement, but Rosalind was too busy basking in the knowledge that he had wanted her home. Her father had wanted her home! She had never been truly alone. He had cared. It was balm for her wounded heart, and a dam burst there and spilled all the hurt away. Her father still loved her. She was flooded with humble gratitude.

The others hung on the Earl's every word. "Yes, a traitor." He nodded for emphasis. "He was bitterly jealous of Arthur Wellesley's elevation to Duke of Wellington—considered it a personal slight. Finally he began to think of England as his enemy. I pitied him—thought him unhinged."

The Earl snorted. "Fool again! I thought that I was helping an old comrade in arms by keeping him near me." He looked up at them fiercely. "He stayed because it gave him a *pied-à-terre* here on the coast. The dog! As one of England's respected generals, he had easy entry to the War Office and living at Summerfields gave him equally easy access to France." He shook his head and winced slightly at the pain the movement caused him. "I never suspected a thing." He shot a look at young Lord Winston. "So take no offense that I call your father fool. He has a rival for the title in me."

Cook arrived with a bowl of water and clean cloths to care for his wound. Summerfield waved her away. "Bitwell's the task at hand. We must stop him. He's hellbent on rescuing Radley before they get him to London to talk." He darted a measuring look at Perseus. "If he can't win him free, likely he'll silence him. Either way could be touchy for Moreland and that Lieutenant."

"We must hurry! We must help them!" Valerie, wringing her hands helplessly, ran in a little circle, then subsided, her eyes huge in her face.

"Do you know where Bitwell may be?" Rosalind asked.

"No, but I know where he plans his ambush. He told me where he'd head them off just before he shot me."

"Shot you!" Rosalind was as white as death.

Her father chuckled as he levered himself out of his chair. "Just a slight graze, girl." He touched his wound lightly. "But I'd be a sorry old soldier if I didn't have the sense to play dead when needful. Lucky for me head wounds bleed like the very devil." He opened his arms, and Rosalind flew into them. Clasping her to his chest, he spoke to Perseus over her head. "We'll need pistols and a map, Lord Winston."

Perseus ran to get the required items, while Rosalind and her father stood savoring their reunion and Valerie paced the hall like a madwoman.

Perseus returned and spread the map of the area out on a table. "Here, sir."

"This is the point of ambush." Summerfield touched the map.

Perseus groaned. "How much of a lead does he have?"

"He shot me at half past four and left the house ten minutes later."

"We'll never be in time. We can't make up an hour's head start!" Perseus was appalled.

The Earl disappeared and the General spoke: "Chin up, Winston! With your sloop to shortcut to this point"—he swept his finger across the chart— "we should be in time. What can you muster in the way of men?"

"There's me and the Green boys we're using as footmen."

"And me!" Valerie cried as she rushed back into the room. "I must be of some use." Her eyes were pleading. "I *cannot* stay behind."

Rosalind added quietly, "I still remember how to shoot, Father."

Her parent beamed at her. "And a fine eye you always had, girl."

Perseus was aghast. "You can't mean you intend to let them come?"

The General looked at him sardonically. "You say you have only the Greens. They're no good to me, as I know for a fact neither can shoot. And I seriously doubt they'll be any use to you if you intend to deploy them to keep the ladies at home."

One look at the determination on the faces of the two women convinced Perseus his neighbor was correct. He sighed in defeat. "I suppose I should be grateful the Gemini haven't signed on." He scooped up two boxes containing two sets of matching dueling pistols—works of art by Manton—grabbed his long fowling piece and started for the door.

Snatching cloaks from Cassie as she joined them carrying three, the ladies, led by the General, hurried out the door after him while Cook wailed lamentations in the great hall.

Getting everyone out to the *Windmaiden* in the tiny dinghy would take two trips. The Gemini arrived as Rosalind and her father waited and insisted on going along.

The General distracted the boys by sending them to fetch his pistols from his saddle holsters.

"Father!" His ploy had Rosalind's heart in her throat. The thought of the Gemini with loaded pistols was not contemplable.

"Stand easy, girl." He pulled aside his ancient long-skirted coat and showed her the pistols safe in his possession.

Before the eager twins had gotten halfway back up the path, there was shower of rock from the top, and a breathless Andromeda, cloak flying and dark curls in disarray, skidded down to where they stood. "I just got back from my errand in the village. Cook told me the most extraordinary story! I'm coming, too. I can help Perseus sail the sloop." She looked around the group with bright-eyed confidence.

Summerfield glared at her, and Perseus, arriving back with the dinghy at just that moment, was forced to say, "It's true, sir. Andy's a good sailor." He scowled at his sister, resentful at having had to praise her.

"Yes, I am," Andy assured him. "I can do anything with a boat that Perseus can do."

"Not bloody likely!" her brother growled rudely.

Summerfield ignored the glaring young Winstons—he'd always thought them a quarrelsome lot of brats. "Very well. Let's get on with it, then."

They all scrambled to obey the General's order.

Minutes later the *Windmaiden* left her anchorage to the sound of two desperately disappointed nine-year-olds spilling heedlessly down the path vigorously protesting at being left behind. All on board pretended neither to see nor hear them as the wind caught the sails and strongly moved the fleet sloop on her way. With a brisk wind astern, they fairly flew over the water.

Rosalind began to believe they would be in time to prevent bloodshed, and started to breathe again. Andromeda and Perseus nursed every inch of speed from the swift craft, while Rosalind sat huddled on the forward deck with Cassie and

Valerie, the box of primed and loaded dueling pistols Perseus had given her safe in her lap.

The knowledge that she *would* shoot to save Moreland sat heavily on her conscience. She was glad she was a good shot. Perhaps she would not kill her target. There was no doubt in her mind, however, that she would shoot Bitwell down like a dog if it were the only way she could save Moreland.

Chapter 26

The moon was on the rise by the time they reached their destination. With the wind fair astern, the sloop had made excellent time. Within the hour they reached the point the General had chosen to go ashore.

As they anchored *Windmaiden* and were preparing to ferry themselves ashore, Perseus suddenly stopped lowering the dinghy and threw up a hand. Instantly all activity ceased and they were frozen still as they strained, breathless, to hear whatever sound had alerted him. Borne on the shifting night wind came a faint jingle of harness and the pounding of hooves.

"Moreland's carriage!" the General cried. "Hurry!"

Rosalind felt her fingernails bite into her palms.

Andromeda saw the strain on her face and gave her a shove. "Go with them." She looked intently at her sister-in-law. "I know you love him. Go!"

Rosalind gave her a grateful hug, gathered her

191

skirts, and slipped over the side into the dinghy. After one look at her face, neither Perseus nor her father forbade her to come with them.

"I'll hold the ship!" Andromeda promised dramatically from her place at the rail.

"*We'll* hold the ship," Cassie amended, shoving up beside her. She carried Perseus's fowling piece, its long barrel gleaming in the moonlight.

"God speed," Valerie whispered to them as the crowded dinghy pulled away. Her knuckles were white as she clenched the rail. Deeply fearful for her brother and terrified that Lytton might be harmed, she was untouched by the high excitement the other two girls left aboard felt. She took it as her part to pray.

Perseus pulled strongly at the oars, and soon the hull of their small craft grated on the shingle of the beach. The men piled out of the boat and pulled it high on the shore where Rosalind disembarked dry shod.

Stumbling frequently in the moon-cast shadows, they struggled to the roadway. Once on the road, they could see in the distance the sidelights of Moreland's traveling coach. They hurried to meet it, feeling keenly the absence of horses. Before Rosalind could form a prayer of thanksgiving that they were in time to warn Moreland, shots rang out on the night air.

They saw the coach slew to a halt, horses plunging, as Gates fell from the box clutching his shoulder. Then Moreland threw himself out of the coach, firing at an attacker as he ran toward cover.

One of the others spurred his horse savagely forward. Bitwell, his fury-twisted face briefly illuminated by a side lamp, sent his horse charging after the Viscount. The shot from his pistol cracked loud in the quiet night.

Horses reared in their traces, frantic at the pistol shots and the smell of blood. Rosalind's anguished cry was lost in their shrill neighing as she flung herself toward the spot where Moreland had fallen. She was heedless of her own safety as she ran to his side, the box of dueling pistols clamped to her chest, forgotten.

"Moreland!" She saw him struggling to rise. Her frantic cry as she fell to her knees beside the man she loved alerted the man she had scorned. With a mad cry of rage Bitwell pulled his second pistol and pointed it straight at Rosalind's slender back.

"No!" Moreland roared as he grabbed Rosalind into a crushing embrace with his right arm. He twisted his body to shield hers. The box she carried ground into his chest, startling him. He looked at it blankly, then threw her to the ground and crouched in front of her, attempting to shield her as he scrabbled fiercely to open the box one-handed, his wounded left arm dangling uselessly.

Time had tumbled into long slow seconds that each seemed to last forever. Moreland could see Bitwell adjust his aim—not at him. Oh, God! At Rosalind!

Moreland shifted position frantically, attempting to take the ball himself, but he knew he would be too late. In the slowed-down world that contained them, there was not going to be enough time!

Suddenly, with a look of comic surprise, Bitwell threw up his hands and slowly toppled from his saddle. His pistol discharged, the ball plowing harmlessly into the turf next to Moreland's knee.

Behind Bitwell, haggard in the moonlight, General Summerfield stood with smoking weapon. His face was that of both executioner and mourner.

Moreland snatched Rosalind to him and crushed her mouth in a frantic kiss, as heedless of those around him as he was that his own blood soaked the back of her gown. "My love! He would have killed you!" He looked at her, bewildered and fiercely protective.

"Ah, but he did not." Rosalind cared nothing for her own recent peril. Moreland was safe. Truly God heard unspoken prayers. He was safe! She leaned against him and wonderingly touched the back of her hand to her bruised lips.

While Lytton and Perseus bound the wound in Gates's shoulder and assisted him into the coach for delivery to the nearest doctor, Rosalind gently inspected the arm she had seen Moreland fail to use, and gasped to see the blood.

"Let me look at that," the General demanded. He seized the fabric of Moreland's sleeve at the hole the ball had made and ripped it quickly away from the wound.

"Oh, blast," Moreland said weakly, "I think I . . . am going to . . ." His sentence unfinished, Moreland pitched forward in a faint.

Summerfield caught him and eased him gently to the ground. Taking advantage of the younger man's swoon, he thoroughly examined the wound. Satisfied that it was a clean one, the General bound it tightly. "He's lucky. The ball went clean through.

Never touched a bone. He'll be right as a trivet in a couple of weeks."

He sat back on his heels, satisfied with his work and grateful for something to take his mind off the still body of his one-time friend and comrade-in-arms.

"Father," Rosalind said softly.

"What is it, girl?"

She blushed as she sought words. "If you would, please, I'd rather he not know just yet that we are related."

The General looked at her hard. He had no need to ask which *he* she meant. Merging his bushy gray eyebrows at the bridge of his nose in a fierce frown, he growled, "What's afoot, minx?"

Moreland groaned and stirred. Rosalind put a finger to her lips, her eyes pleading. The General, his own eyes narrowed in concentration, finally nodded, and Rosalind smiled at him radiantly before turning her complete attention to her fallen beloved.

"I feel a perfect fool," Moreland said groggily. He was embarrassed to have lost consciousness over so minor a wound.

"Handled you a bit roughly, is all. Apologize." The General glared down at him, daring him to agree.

Moreland had been among too many politicians to fall into that trap. He avoided it neatly. "Thank you for your help, sir." He grinned at Summerfield boyishly. "I wonder if I might trouble you for a hand up?"

He had hit just the right note. Rosalind's father

shot her an approving glance and solicitously helped the Viscount to his feet.

Moreland thanked him gravely, then said, "I can guess from what has just occurred that we have much to say to each other, General. You have my gratitude. May I call on you when I return from delivering my prisoner to London?"

Summerfield bowed. "My pleasure." He looked from Lytton to Moreland. "I'll lend you Winston to drive. I can manage the sloop with Andromeda." He spoke with the assurance of long familiarity with Andromeda's abilities on a boat.

A little dazed, Moreland didn't notice the variation on his butler's name. His mind was on a more important matter. He turned to draw Rosalind forward. "This is my housekeeper, sir." He didn't notice the General bristling, as his gaze was locked with Rosalind's. "She is dearer to me than life. I would appreciate it if you would see her safely back to Castle Winston."

The General turned scarlet with the effort he was making to obey his daughter's eyes. Finally he snorted. "Castle Madcap is more like, if you ask me! But aye. I'll see the wench safely home." He spun on his heel and stomped away back toward the beach and the *Windmaiden*. "Come along . . . *Housekeeper!*" he growled.

Chapter 27

Rosalind took Moreland's letter to the terrace where he had last stood with her at Castle Winston. She was smiling as she passed through the library's French doors onto the sun-washed flagstones. Even the day was smiling, pouring sunshine down on her as she crossed to touch with caressing fingers the very spot on the seaward wall against which he had leaned.

She put her back against his place on the wall and pretended the sun-washed stones still held his warmth. Blushing, she imagined his fierce embrace and touched her lips, remembering his kisses.

"Ah! There you are. I've been looking for you all over." Andromeda bounced out of the library and came to Rosalind's side. "Perseus told me you had a letter from Moreland, and I wanted to know what it said." She looked a little startled. "Oh, dear, that was rather rude!" She grinned and shrugged away

her apology. "Did he find anyone else involved in
Bitwell's spy ring?"

Rosalind smiled at her impetuous young sister-
in-law. "No. At least, if he did, he didn't write about
it."

"What did he say, then?" Andromeda caught the
hesitant expression that crossed Rosalind's face.
Instantly she was all excitement. "Oh, Roz! Did he
make you an offer?"

Rosalind smiled. She looked again at his letter.
How imperious he was! How commanding! Here in
her hand was her lord and master telling her where
and when he would condescend to marry her. Such
confidence that she would obey—it showed in
every stroke of his pen.

"He has commanded me to the altar, rather."

"What? Like a master to his slave?" Andromeda
didn't find that very romantic.

Rosalind nodded.

"You'll never let him get away with such behavior! The very idea. Who would have thought he'd
behave so discourteously?" Andromeda fumed.

Rosalind laughed. Though the prospect of marrying Moreland more than pleased her, she had no
intention of allowing such high-handedness. "You
are absolutely right, Andy. If I let him get away with
this and do nothing to take him down a peg or two,
my life will surely be a misery!" Her eyes twinkled.
Rosalind had no intention of letting any part of her
life with Moreland be miserable. "I am formulating
a plan. Will you and the others take part in it?"

"Oh, yes! I am sure I can speak for us all."

"Good. Leave me to polish the details of my little

surprise. You go and tell the others to be prepared to take part."

"What fun. Come and tell us the whole when you have decided what must be done." In a flurry of skirts Andromeda ran back into the house to find and alert the rest of the Winstons.

Left alone, Rosalind chose a bench set in a protected alcove opposite a low part of the wall that allowed its occupant a view of the sea. Seating herself comfortably, she musingly contemplated the blue sparkle of the sunlit Channel. Absently tapping the edge of his precious letter gently against her lips, she planned her beloved Moreland's mild comeuppance.

Moreland seethed with impatience as the last reports on his operation were being gone over at the War Office. Now that he had made the decision to marry his housekeeper—very well, the Winstons' housekeeper—he was in a fever to do so. Every moment apart from her stretched into what seemed hours. He was short-tempered in the extreme and kept his demeanor acceptable to those around him only with the greatest effort.

To his longtime friend, Gates, who was recuperating nicely from the wound in his shoulder, he let the true state of his mind—and his suspicions about the Winston 'servants'—be known. Without Gates, he felt he might have abandoned his duty and galloped madly to Castle Winston.

Gates had sputtered a bit when he'd shared the good news with him. That was only natural; he was, in addition to being a friend, a family retainer, after all, and could not like the idea of him renouncing his title to marry a servant. But damned if Moreland understood why his valet had thrown back his head and laughed like a jackass. Perhaps it amused him to think of the Winstons playing servants.

Gates did make Moreland the gift of a piece of precious information—one that left the Viscount with the warm certainty he was doing the right thing in giving up the trappings of nobility to marry his love. Gates told him why *she* had not had on her wedding ring when he'd first seen her at that long-ago campfire. "I learned from my friend MacFie that she'd sold her wedding band to get money to buy medicine for him. MacFie would not have survived without it. He thinks her an angel." If only she could have been a Winston, too, how simple it would be. But there were no auburn-haired Winstons, to his sorrow. There was only one blond Winston as far as he'd heard. All the other Winstons were dark-haired and had been for generations.

"Thank you, John," Moreland said from a suddenly tight throat. Gates's words were more to him than could be the richest wedding present. He wondered why he felt Gates had started to tell him more.

Now, except for the delay that seemed inevitable when dealing with the War Office, Moreland had but one fly in his ointment.

His plans for the wedding were complete. The vicar of the little church by the sea had agreed to perform the ceremony. The flowers from his hot-house at More Park were even on their way to transform the church into a fairy bower for his beloved's special day. Deep in his pocket he guarded the special license he had procured to make the marriage possible so quickly. Valerie and Lytton, though they both warned him he would be placing his social life in grave jeopardy, had agreed to be present.

There remained but a single problem—one that had caused the bishop's secretary a moment of distress. *He still didn't know her first name! Rose*, he had written finally. No other words. He vowed to fill the rest in later.

The day dawned bright and clear. Moreland waited at the church in a state of high anxiety.

Having to wait with a prelate who regarded him with some disfavor upon learning he was not in possession of his bride's first name did nothing to improve things for him. On top of that, he was prey to misgivings that had never crossed his mind hitherto. Suppose she did not come, God forbid! It didn't bear thinking on! Her silence, however, unnerved him.

Thank God the courier had assured him she'd received his letter personally, otherwise . . . That, too, did not stand up well to his thinking on it. His palms, perfectly dry through episodes in which he had been in mortal danger, were suddenly damp.

Always cool and correct in all matters sartorial, the Viscount could not resist the urge to run his fingers under the edge of a cravat that had mysteriously grown too snug. Just when he was sure he would bolt from the vicar's side, the door at the foot of the aisle opened.

On a breath of fresh salt air, a magnificently

dressed young man regally entered. Moreland watched him as he was ushered past birdlike Miss Evans where she sat smiling between Cook and Tom Coachman near the back of the church, up to the pew reserved for centuries exclusively for the Earls of Winston. Thinking he should have found time to inspect that portrait of the deceased sixth Earl, he realized his butler was indeed the eighth. He returned Perseus's smile with a twinkle in his eye, glad the masquerade was ended.

The door opened again, and a crowd of lightly cloaked women entered, his sister among them, stifling glad laughter. Moreland felt a faint relief that she had reconciled herself to the idea of this marriage.

He saw the tall figure of the Earl of Summerfield and waited for him to join Valerie in the pew to which Lytton escorted her before joining him at the altar, but Summerfield remained at the door.

Then, suddenly, nothing mattered but the woman who took Summerfield's arm. Not the elegantly clad chambermaid who preceded her down the aisle, nor the unexplainably now blond abigail, her brows still faintly dark, that had so ably served his sister. And certainly not the twin boys who, grinning, carried the train of *her* exquisite gown.

That the staff from—yes, Summerfield had called it right—Castle Madcap—each were obviously of the Quality came as no surprise to him and mattered not at all. Only his bride existed for Moreland as their gazes locked, and he saw the calm certainty in her eyes.

She in turn exalted in the love she saw in his.

The entire church party felt their throats constrict to see what passed between these two.

Rosalind and the Earl of Summerfield reached the foot of the altar, and the vicar began the service. When he asked, "Who gives this woman?" General Lord Summerfield stepped forward and passed Rosalind's hand from his own arm to Moreland's. "Her father," the General said in a firm voice fraught with meaning. His eagle glare met Moreland's startled gaze with a vengeance.

Such an electric shock of emotion jolted Moreland at her touch that he merely smiled to hear the Earl's declaration. His joy knew no bounds—his beautiful love was the daughter of an Earl. Vaguely he heard Gates's laughter boom out and be shushed.

Moreland spoke his responses through a smile that lit the altar. He was so deep in contemplation of his bride, he barely heard the vicar when he asked, "Do you, Rosalind Anna . . ."

Moreland, drowning in her eyes, lost in the maelstom of his love for her, heard only "Rosalind." *Rosalind!* He smiled radiantly down at the treasured woman at his side.

At last he knew her first name! Given permission by the prelate, he took *Rosalind* tenderly in his arms and kissed her gently.

She smiled up at him when he released her, and all the assembled company saw his bewildered delight—Rosalind's gentle revenge.

Later in the vestry, when the married couple and all their friends had departed, the clergyman carefully altered the single word "Rose" on the special license. It was only a moment's work to change the *e* to *a* and write all the rest.

He shook his white head slightly and sighed. It would never cease to amaze him, this dreadful carelessness of the nobility.